MERCURY MAN

MERCURY MAN

Tom Henighan

A BOARDWALK BOOK
A MEMBER OF THE DUNDURN GROUP
TORONTO

Editor: Barry Jowett
Copy-Editor: Jennifer Bergeron
Design: Jennifer Scott
Printer: Transcontinental

National Library of Canada Cataloguing in Publication Data

Henighan, Tom
   Mercury man/Tom Henighan.

ISBN 1-55002-508-2

I. Title.

PS8565.E582M47 2004   jC813'.54   C2004-901391-2

1   2   3   4   5   08   07   06   05   04

 Conseil des Arts du Canada   Canada Council for the Arts   Canada   ONTARIO ARTS COUNCIL
CONSEIL DES ARTS DE L'ONTARIO

We acknowledge the support of the **Canada Council for the Arts** and the **Ontario Arts Council** for our publishing program. We also acknowledge the financial support of the **Government of Canada** through the **Book Publishing Industry Development Program** and **The Association for the Export of Canadian Books**, and the **Government of Ontario** through the **Ontario Book Publishers Tax Credit** program.

Printed and bound in Canada.✪   Printed on recycled paper.   www.dundurn.com

Dundurn Press
8 Market Street
Suite 200
Toronto, Ontario, Canada
M5E 1M6

Gazelle Book Services Limited
White Cross Mills
Hightown, Lancaster, England
LA1 4X5

Dundurn Press
2250 Military Road
Tonawanda NY
U.S.A. 14150

To Rick and Dale Taylor

"Mercury? Oh, sure, that's the Roman name for the Greek god Hermes. That guy was something special! Divine messenger, trickster and the god of businessmen — and thieves — he knew all the paths and portals that lead from world to world, and he could get from here to there in a twinkle. When he put on his travelling hat and winged sandals it meant change was coming, and that could sometimes be painful, although now and then it worked out all right."

— Martin Seeland,
Conversations on Mythology

CHAPTER ONE

Heat Wave

Tom Blake struggled to the window. For two weeks the city had boiled and baked in the July weather. All along Morris Street, a ruler-straight passage through the labyrinth of Mechanicstown, the pavement radiated heat. Light glared from the buildings opposite and from the tops of the parked cars, dazzling the boy's eyes.

He squinted and leaned over the sill, trying to find a breeze in the steamy air. He was sweating badly, attempting to ignore the smells that sifted up through the floors of their ancient, run-down apartment block. Garbage smells, cigarette smoke, hints of overcooked food, and human sweat. The smell of time and waste, of lost hopes and stagnant purposes — after a while he couldn't stand them any more and pulled away from the window. He looked around in despair, then lumbered to the door.

There was nowhere to go, but anywhere was better than here. He grabbed his key from the hook and took a last look around the place. A living room stuffed with second-hand furniture from Valuemart, the faded walls posted with family photographs, a few old copies of *Heavy Metal* lying on the tattered rug where he had dropped them after falling asleep. If he and his mother had only been able to find a portable fan it might have been bearable, but fans at a price they could pay were impossible to locate in this heat wave. His mother worked in an air-conditioned supermarket all day, and he had his spell at the diner; otherwise it would have been unbearable.

Wiping his sweating forehead, Tom thought of Grandpa Sandalls. He tramped down the stairs and stepped into the street. Grandpa Sandalls's place had air conditioning, and they had slept there a couple of nights — his mother in the spare room and he on the couch — but Grandpa had a way of getting touchy when you stuck around too long. He was great for an hour or so, then his energy seemed to fade and you sensed that he had no use for you, that he wanted to make you disappear.

Still, an hour in the air conditioning would help. And there would be a cold drink, some snacks, and his collections to check out, including the fabulous comic books …

Tom walked west toward the Hollis Street intersection. Hollis was a little wider and much busier than Morris Street. In one direction it led to the river, where the old warehouses crowded together along the smelly and polluted channel. Going the other way you could reach Pitt Park, beyond which lay suburban homes, the library, and city hall. Mechanicstown formed a pocket of shabby buildings and cheap stores in the heart of the city. Even so, it was not really convenient to anything and was serviced only by a single hopeless bus route. Committees were always suggesting that the area (which was one of the city's oldest) should be modernized and improved, but nothing was ever done.

Tom strolled along the street, beginning to get thirsty already. He wondered where Pete and the guys were. Bim, he knew, would be in the country at his uncle's farm. He hadn't seen Estella Lopez in days. Old men and old women were everywhere — the rents were quite low in Mechanicstown. All around him, the shabby trees seemed withered, and cats hid in the darkest alleys. Yet a couple of geezers, with canes and sunglasses, tottered along past the fire hydrant, casting wistful glances at its locked-up metal. Maybe they were remembering the torrents of clear water that had been released by a merciful authority on some long-vanished summer day. Maybe they were afraid they would fall asleep and die if they didn't move.

On the corner of Hollis Tom hesitated. It was an anonymous intersection at the best of times, and today the action was minimal — one or two delivery trucks, a few cyclists dressed as if they were heading for the beach, and an empty bus bumping down from the Pitt Park area.

Tom stood looking around at the stores. Small stores, with cheap gaudy signs and dark interiors — they were always changing hands, always offering something new that nobody wanted. How did people think they could make a living selling "barely used" clothes, gaudy amateur artwork, or ten-year-old knick-knacks for bathrooms? Almost nobody ever dropped in on such places, and only the bar at the corner, the magazine shop, and the economy branch of a local funeral home survived the constant changes.

"Hey, man, you lookin' for a freezer locker or something?"

The figure was upon him before he could blink: Jeff Parker the jogging fool, stripped down and sweating, pumping his feet up and down, smiling, dancing around.

"You must be crazy! Some day to be in motion," Tom said, smiling. He was flattered to be addressed by Jeff, a high school superstar who had won every race he had ever entered and was being courted by track coaches from all over the country.

"I'm in training, I'm always in training. Beat the heat, get in shape for the meet — you know how it is. You headed for work?"

"Not today. Gotta go check on my grandfather — he's getting pretty old. Besides, he's got air conditioning, and I nearly fried in our apartment."

"Sounds like a cool move. You ought to be in motion, though. Don't get any benefit just lumbering around the streets, like."

Even as he spoke, Jeff himself stayed in motion, his strong legs pumping steadily. Now he danced around Tom, who had to keep turning to face him. Jeff was a strong guy, shorter than Tom but with well-developed chest and arms. His legs, not really long, were awesomely moulded. He was bare to the waist and sweating like a pig.

"You look like you could run, man. How come you never tried? Always wondered about you, Blake. I may have to recruit you as a partner. Just tried to haul up Wally Jones, but he looks something like a zombie. Must have been out drinking or got something up his nose. Wanna jog back to the park with me?"

"Sorry, Jeff. Got to go on to my grandfather's."

"Hey, then, you wanna play Little Red Riding Hood, you go ahead." Jeff smiled at him. "I don't see no basket, but you watch out for the wolf!"

He whirled away and with a few strong strides disappeared down Morris Street.

Almost without looking, Tom scampered across the intersection. A horn sounded close by. His pace continued fast — he didn't look around. He felt the sweat run but didn't let that slow him down.

Of course he could run! He was amazed and a little irritated by Jeff's taunting. Sure, it was flattering. To run with Jeff Parker — some kids would kill for the privilege. It sounded too much like his mother, though. "Don't know why you don't take up some sport," she would say to him. "Just look at you, rangy and strong, the figure of a tennis star. You never play baseball or anything. Watching too much TV again — I wish you'd get out and get active!"

Tom winced at the memory, swore at a cat that refused to move from a hot patch of sidewalk, dodged a kid on a bicycle, and walked on past the small hardware stores, the tailor, and the bakery.

Of course his mother would always be sorry after one of her lectures and give him credit for his hard work and study. In first-year high he had even won a prize. It was for an essay entitled "Reaching for the Stars," which had been read by one of his friends to the assembled city schools because he was too scared to do it. His mother was thrilled; she knew it didn't come easy to him. Books didn't grab him — he liked movies much better — but when he had to, he could buckle down.

There was no competition with dating and parties, either, because he wasn't into that scene — avoided it like poison, in fact. Tom told himself he didn't want any part of it, yet he got angry when he overheard his mother telling someone he was "shy."

The hell with them all, he was glad he was on the way to Grandpa's.

But that crack about Little Red Riding Hood stuck in his head. Come to think of it, he hadn't brought anything for the old man.

He shook his head. Two blocks more and I've had it, he thought. Jeff must be out of his mind, running around in this weather. Tom jingled the change in his pockets, considering whether he should stop for a coke. But why waste the money when he was almost there?

He crossed another intersection, sped up past the fire station. (His father, who had run off with another woman when Tom was ten, had been a fireman. Neither he nor his mother had heard from him in years.)

Up ahead, Tom was relieved to see the flashing metal roof and the hulking brown walls of the oversized private house where his grandfather rented a small apartment. The place, a shabby former mansion, was owned by a couple of old women who liked having a man on the premises. Tom thought it was more like an old folks' home than anything, tucked among a block of semi-detached anonymous rabbit warrens — "affordable housing," as they advertised it — and right behind an old brewery, but his grandfather didn't seem to mind. "Swore I'd never take an apartment," Jack Sandalls boasted. "Can't stand elevators and dinky little mailboxes and people thumping overhead and cooking cabbage down the hall. And as for those boxes over there!" — here he would point to the rabbit warrens — "I'd die in one of those places!"

Jack was a retired sea captain who had gambled and lost most of his life savings, yet he had salted away enough money to keep himself well stocked with booze and tobacco — and quite a few other things besides. Occasionally he helped out his daughter — he had paid for Tom's computer, in fact, though it wasn't a very up-to-date model — and he had once treated them to a modest vacation. He thought Tom should be an artist because he could draw so well — another undeveloped talent that had caused Tom nothing but trouble.

Now he hustled down the path as the old metal gate clanked shut behind him. He marched past the honeysuckle and the lilac bushes, dry as old sticks and bare of blooms. He cast a glance at the high curtained first-floor windows and thought he saw one of the old ladies peering out at him, but — anxious to avoid them — he dodged around the side of the house, thumped up the wooden stairs, and rang the bell of Grandpa's door.

Footsteps sounded inside; he heard his grandfather's familiar muttered curses, then the door opened and the old man stood before him, unshaven, with a ragged mop of silver hair. Just turning seventy, Jack Sandalls was stocky and plump, with a ruddy, weather-beaten face and a jolly bulbous nose. He had big meaty hands that had steered many a ship safely into harbour. Just then, however, he was dressed in a green bathrobe that made him look like a retired boxer. He waved Tom inside readily enough, although his expression was serious, almost grim.

"I thought you were coming yesterday," he said. His grey eyes looked a little bleary, from drink, maybe, or from lack of sleep.

"Sorry, Granddad, they called me to work all of a sudden. You know how it is, they fire you if you turn them down too much."

Jack sniffed, but seemed to relent.

"Come in, kid. I figured that was it. The ladies baked a chicken pie for us and I got some left. I guess you're hungry as well as hot."

Tom stepped into the familiar front room, which reeked of tobacco and unwashed socks. The air conditioning was wonderful, though, a grinding mercy in the background that made him shiver once and then forget about the heat.

Tom loved his grandfather's place, though his mother mildly disapproved. There were books and magazines everywhere, huge overstuffed chairs, an enormous sofa, a worn oriental rug. A few prints of racing sloops decorated the walls, and a table along one wall was covered with old navigation gear and other sea items — sextants and small spyglasses, a hook from an ancient anchor, brass fittings, dishes stamped with the names of famous ships, pieces of sailcloth, compasses and barometers, maps and charts.

He followed Jack down the hall and into the large kitchen. It was untidy as always, but welcoming. An old cookstove occupied one wall, and there was a view of the overgrown jungle of the backyard.

"Got the pie in the oven to warm up. Help yourself to an Orangina. Got something new to show you today."

Tom sat at the table and finished off a bottle of Orangina while his grandfather retreated to his bedroom. He returned carrying a big envelope, already opened, out of which he pulled a slipcase enclosing some comic books.

"This is going to blow you away," he said, almost clucking with pleasure. Tom knew how much pride his grandfather took in his comic book collection. It occupied one whole wall of his bedroom and contained many golden age classics. It was "one of the best," as the old man said, and he always added, "A hundred thousand bucks wouldn't touch it," which Tom and his mother were certain was an exaggeration.

"Just got these yesterday from Tokyo. Had to put out more than I figured to, but what the hell — they're unique!"

Jack opened up the slipcase and carefully set the comics on the table. There were only four of them, part of a series, and although they seemed to be in mint condition there was something dated about them, perhaps due to the cheap paper and the somewhat old-fashioned style of the drawings. Tom picked one up and it felt frail in his hands, but the cover was confident and bright.

"MERCURY MAN COMICS," it announced. And there, underneath, was Mercury Man himself, in all his glory. A bright caped figured leaping across the page at a cowering twisted-faced Nazi gunman. The date and price stamp read: August, 1941, Vol I, Number 1. 10 cents.

"I never heard of Mercury Man," Tom said.

"Of course you haven't!" Jack snapped. "These are among the few issues ever printed, and just think, by golly, I have 'em!"

"They must be worth a lot," Tom said. He was taking in Mercury Man's costume: blue tights, a red top emblazoned with a staff and snakes, a red hood, a blue cape, and winged slippers instead of boots.

"Isn't he a bit of a rip-off of The Flash?" Tom wondered aloud. Thanks to his grandfather, he knew a lot about the golden age comic heroes.

"Not really. The Flash had blue trousers with yellow streaks down the side. He had the Mercury helmet, sure, and the winged slippers, but the big thing is that he could go so fast you couldn't see him. Now Mercury Man is different: he can't go into high-speed motion, but he just has to touch that staff on his chest with three fingers of his left hand and he can change into almost anything he wants. When they try to shoot him he could turn into a mouse, for example."

"Not a good move," Tom said.

"Or he could turn into a lion or a tiger and scare the snot out of them!"

"You have to be careful what you change into," Tom said. He remembered reading stories about some unfortunate changes.

"Of course you do! But Mercury Man isn't a fool. His alter ego is Oliver Graham; he lectures on mythology at Lincoln University — that's how he found the old book that gave him the formula for becoming Mercury Man. You see he travelled to Thessaly in Greece — a place known for its witchcraft — and in a tiny mountain village —"

"Sure, sure …"

Jack held up the first comic. "MERCURY MAN FIGHTS A NAZI PLOT TO BLOW UP THE EMPIRE STATE BUILDING!"

"Neat, huh?"

"Nazis? Pretty corny."

Grandpa Sandalls scowled. "The trouble with you kids today is that you're all too skeptical. It goes with being lazy and with thinking you know everything. You wouldn't even *care* if Nazi spies blew up the Empire State Building."

Tom studied the face of the spy that was crumpling under the impact of Mercury Man's gloved fist. He thought to himself: *Maybe I wouldn't care …*

"Of course I would, Grandpa. It would be terrorists, though, or neo-Nazis. This is so … out of date."

"That's the point, kid! It's historical. And don't qualify everything to death! Some things are best taken in a gulp."

Bad-tasting things, Tom wanted to say, but he knew better than to push his grandfather too far.

"So it's the date that makes these valuable, right, Grandpa? And the mint condition?"

"It's all that, Tom, but it's something else. You see, most comics were created in Metropolis itself, in the original Gotham City. You know what I mean? New York cornered the market in this field like it did for almost everything. But there were some exceptions. Like Mercury Man. You know where Mercury Man was created and printed? You'll never guess, I'll wager that."

"I don't know. L.A., maybe?"

Jack harrumphed mightily and shook his head. "Not a chance! In fact, these little babies were made right here in West Hope. Yes, sir! They were a crazy dream on the part of one of our local characters, a schoolteacher of mine, he was, by name of Marvin Cormer."

"Wow! That *is* amazing."

Tom was thumbing carefully through the comic. Sure enough, even a few of the ads had West Hope addresses. It was almost unheard of.

"This place wasn't always the back of beyond, you know. It had signs of spunk, once. Marvin was a bright guy and a good artist who got fed up with school teaching, and since he knew a lot about the Greek and Roman myths he decided to try to launch his own comic, based on the god Mercury. As you can see for yourself, the product was very good. DC Comics got wind of it and was debating whether to sue him or buy him out when he was drafted. After that the whole thing went on hold, only Marvin didn't come back; he was killed at the Battle of the Bulge."

"And that was the end of Mercury Man Comics."

"That was it, except that I remembered these issues. As a teenager I was stupid enough to trade mine away and it's taken me decades to find them again. I'll never sell them now, not if I starve because of it. They'll be with me when I die, I can tell you."

"I don't know if I feel that way about anything, Grandpa."

Jack shot him a piercing glance. "Time for some pie, I guess. You can look at the comics, but keep them away from the food and drink."

While his grandfather set the table, Tom flipped through the comics. They were very slick, but with a few interesting touches, places where the hero broke out of his frame and smashed a grinning spy with a fist that was larger than life. At the same time, his adventures seemed pretty familiar. After saving the Panama Canal from a Japanese assault team, he was on his way to prevent a super-U-boat attack on the Statue of Liberty.

Mercury Man's most formidable enemy was Dr. Dark, a hideously evil genius whose life had changed for the worse after he'd been scarred by the experimental chemicals he worked with. Mercury Man wasn't completely invincible — none of the superheroes was. In one adventure Dr. Dark learned that Mercury Man could be made helpless by dousing him with mercury. Luckily, as they were about to unmask the helpless hero, Mercury Man's sidekick, Tom Strong — a high school kid whose life Mercury Man had once saved — arrived to rescue him.

"Want gravy with your pie?" Jack called out.

"Sure," Tom managed to reply, although his attention had been suddenly caught by a page of ads at the back of one of the comics.

"SEND AWAY FOR MERCURY MAN'S OWN RING," one of the grubby boxed-in notices read. It pictured a boy, bent over and staring at his own hand. "WITH THE MERCURY MIRROR HIDDEN IN THIS RING YOU'LL BE ABLE TO FOOL YOUR FRIENDS. USE IT TO SEE BEHIND YOU. HIDE MESSAGES INSIDE. LIKE MERCURY MAN, YOU'LL FIND A THOUSAND USES FOR THIS HANDSOME RING. JUST SEND THIS COUPON WITH 25 CENTS AND WE'LL RUSH YOUR OWN PERSONAL MERCURY RING. MONEY BACK GUARANTEE!"

Tom shook his head and smiled. But he noticed that the ad gave a local address: Mercury Enterprises, Second Floor, 221 Harbour Street, West Hope.

Harbour Street — he knew where that was all right.

"OK, so sit down and let's eat!" Jack said.

He stood up quickly. No, it was ridiculous.

"I told you those comics were good," Jack said. "It's got hold of you, I see, despite your cynical ways. What's that you're looking at like a zombie there?"

Tom closed the comic quickly and moved to the table. "Nothing, Grandpa. Let's eat."

"Careful now. We'll just put my treasures over here on the table. Don't want them all splattered with ketchup and Orangina."

They finished the pie quickly and continued with ice cream and iced coffee. His grandfather lit up a pipe and offered to put on *Treasure of the Sierra Madre*, but Tom explained that he couldn't stay that long. His mother would expect him to be there when she got back from work.

"You know you said Marvin what's-his-name was killed at the Battle of the Bulge, Grandpa?"

"Marvin Cormer, yeah, damn shame. I think he could have made it with Mercury Man. Of course the big companies would have bought him out, or he would have set up shop somewhere else, but he might have put this place on the map, too — you never know. Look how well the computer companies are doing now. Oh well, times change."

"What happened to his equipment and stuff after he died?"

"No idea. He had a wife, but she didn't follow up on any of it. Married the operator of the amusement park right next door — fella by the name of Daniel — an oddball, I guess. Anyway, she died and her husband still lives in the old Mercury House. Can you believe it?

The guy never moved! The park's been shut down for years, though. One of the computer companies is trying to buy him out, I hear, but Daniel has some crazy idea that the dump is worth big money. If he's not careful the city will declare it a nuisance or something and he'll practically have to give it away."

"That isn't Harbour Street, near Boone Jetty?"

"Sure. Just down from Fabricon, the squeaky clean computer folks. Hang on, will you? This cheap tobacco stinks. I've got to find my Sobranie." Jack hustled the lunch plates into the sink and left the room.

Suddenly Tom had an idea: what would happen if he sent away for one of the Mercury Man rings? He knew it was ridiculous, and he wouldn't dare tell his grandfather, who would roar with laughter. But the notion had taken hold of him, and it teased and tempted him for no reason he could think of.

He jumped for the pen on the counter, tore off a piece of paper roll, and scribbled down the Harbour Street address of Mercury Man Comics.

He knew if he sent away he would just be wasting a stamp and the post office might not even send his letter back. Or else it would go to the wrong address, or to the old man in the amusement park, who would probably throw it away. But Tom didn't care, because the idea had suddenly taken hold of him that if he sent to the old address he might find a portal that led into the past!

He knew all about portals — or portholes, as he liked to call them — crossing points where you could go from one world to another. Of course they were just in stories; you wouldn't come across them, except as black holes or some weird aspect of physics. Even so, if they existed in physics they might exist in the world around him, even though no one had ever found one.

Maybe the only way you could find one would be to tap into the right time warp. Without that, you couldn't do a thing. And how would you know if the warp was there unless you tried?

He shoved the scribbled paper into his pocket. *I must be losing my mind,* he thought.

Some mumbling and groaning preceded his grandfather's return to the kitchen.

"Damn it all, where the hell's the Sobranie got to!"

"Want me to go get you some, Grandpa?"

Jack laughed. "Thanks, but you'd have to walk pretty far to get a tin of that stuff."

Tom helped his grandfather wash up the lunch dishes. In the middle of this there was a knocking at the door — one of the old women owners had come about some problem. He heard Jack joking with her in the background. Carefully wiping his wet hand on his cut-offs Tom pulled out the scrap of paper and read the address.

Harbour Street. The old amusement park. And Fabricon Computers. An up-and-coming firm, people said, and its motto was *Read the Future in Us.* Tom winced. He felt suddenly ashamed of his crazy notions, of his thoughts of the past and time warps. With a sigh mostly of relief he crumpled up the paper and threw it into the garbage.

CHAPTER TWO

Weird Kids

When he got back to the apartment Tom found a note pinned to the door. It was from his friend Bim Bavasi.

"Pete told me he got a job," it said. "I need the money and I came back to check it out. Can't spend the whole time shovelling cow dung, can I? See you later."

Tom smiled, but at the same time he was a bit puzzled. Bim back in the city? Complaining about being at his uncle's farm? That didn't make sense at all. His uncle didn't make him work that hard and there was swimming and fishing and shooting squirrels, and, above all, an escape from the heat. There was nothing to do in the city that you couldn't do any time. Bim must have come back because someone was pressuring him — his dad, maybe — to earn some money.

Tom had no real sense of what it would be like to have a dad around. Sometimes when he thought of his own dad taking off like he did, he felt as if he could kill him. But there were times — when he felt free and easy and content — that he was glad not to have anyone around to push him. He saw how some dads leaned on their kids, making life hell over nothing, and he was glad to be out of it, although he knew it made things hard for his mother.

Tom stripped off his shirt, went into the bathroom, and washed his face with cold water. The Mercury Man comics and the magic ring came into his mind. He had thrown away the piece of paper but he remembered the address. Frowning at his own image in the mirror, he thought, *What's the point of having blue eyes with dark hair?* He rubbed his cheeks with his fingertips, checking the acne scars from his bad time, searching for the stubble that never seemed to come. Bim, who was eighteen, was shaving already, making jokes about Tom's baby face. And Tom was always being taken for younger than he was. Even the new kids at Blanchard High looked older than he did.

He stalked out of the bathroom and his eye caught the little table that held the telephone and his mother's notepaper.

Get it over with, a voice from within said. *Who's going to know? If you want to do it, go ahead!*

Tom hesitated, then with a sigh he sat down at the table and began to write out the necessary words: "Please send one Mercury Man Magic Ring. I enclose 25 cents. Yours sincerely, Tom Blake."

He wrote his address on it, stuck a quarter to a piece of cardboard with Scotch Tape, and found an envelope.

He wrote the Harbour Street address on it and stuck on a stamp. Retrieving one of the *Heavy Metal* magazines from the floor, he carefully hid the letter in it.

If there's a porthole, I'll find it, he told himself. He smiled at his own obsession. Maybe he didn't really believe there were such things as portholes, but the idea fascinated him, and the game of trying to find one was irresistible. Tom loved the thrill of pretending. He remembered a few weeks before in the city park, throwing a stone at a tree trunk. *If the stone doesn't hit the trunk I'll die tomorrow*, he had told himself. *My mother will die. Terrorists will take over the world. The planet will be hit by a huge meteor.* He didn't believe any of this, but there was a fascination in pretending. It invested the act of throwing the stone with huge excitement. The throw suddenly took on an awesome significance and put him in touch with supreme power. He was transported to the world of the Greek gods, powers who could change human lives by a single gesture and who made up their own rules about the universe. (When the stone missed, he decided on a best two out of three — a godlike privilege.)

In the tiny kitchen he began to wash up the lunch dishes. This was one of his jobs on his days off. Take out the garbage, sweep the floor, keep the kitchen in decent order — his mother wasn't very demanding. Karen Blake worked five days a week, got home at six, and made dinner for them both. On many days she used the microwave, bringing something from the supermarket, but sometimes she spent an hour doing the cooking. Tom didn't like those times — he was happier with the microwave food — and she was always disappointed when he got impatient or disliked what she fixed for him.

They got on pretty well, although they sometimes had problems. She was always complaining that he never talked to her, but what was he going to talk about? She wouldn't want to hear jokes about sex or any filthy story — which is what the guys passed around — and she wasn't interested in the movies he watched, or in the science fiction books he read. There wasn't much left to get into, really, although they sometimes had talks about his "plans."

"Do you have any plans, Tom?" she would ask, meaning what did he want to be when he was thirty-five, but of course he had no idea.

He was hoping that Grandpa wasn't kidding, that he really had the money to pay for college or university. Of course he didn't know what he wanted to study — it was too soon for that. And there were still some roadblocks up ahead — calculus and economics, for example.

The thought of calculus made him feel a little sick, so he was glad when the phone rang.

"Hi, it's Pete," the voice said. Tom perked up. He and Pete played pool, and he waited for the usual "Wanta go for it?" It didn't come, though. Pete had something else on his mind.

"I got a new job," Pete told him. "Bim might get one, too."

"I can't believe he came back to the city," Tom said. "Where are all these jobs coming from? A new McDonald's?"

"Are you kidding? Those are joe jobs. Naw, this is with Fabricon. Haven't you heard? They're hiring all sorts of kids. Steady work, discounts on computers. It's the greatest. You should go for it — all you have to do is call them."

"I can't believe this. Don't you remember when we tried them at the beginning of the summer? They practically threw us out. They said they only hired through the work-study program. They weren't even friendly."

"Everything's changed. They're looking for high school students now. Not only the nerds — everybody. You should quit that smelly diner and get over there."

"I can't do that. They gave me the job because my grandpa asked them to. I can't just walk out on them."

"Give them two weeks' notice."

"Naw. ... So are we going to a movie tonight?"

"Can't. Gotta go over to Fabricon. There's a presentation. Getting to know the firm. I have to take Bim. Why don't you come? You could get a job. You're crazy to wash dishes in that dump when you can be at Fabricon."

"I told you, I can't. Hey, I hear my mum. Gotta go now. See you tomorrow, Pete."

Tom swung the phone down and made a dash for the kitchen. He'd left the water running in the sink and it was nearly overflowing. He cleaned out the slops, and as the water swooshed away, leaving a pile of half-clean dishes, he heard the door open and his mother call his name.

"Hi, Tommy, you here? I've got someone with me tonight."

Tom stiffened. He turned off the water, ran his hands across a towel, and almost vaulted out of the tiny kitchen.

There stood his mother, smiling uneasily, and beside her, to his dismay, he saw the stocky, bearded figure of Chuck Reichert, the assistant manager of the A&P store where she worked.

Reichert, despite his loosened tie and his rolled-up sleeves, looked uncomfortable and seemed to be sweating heavily. He cradled his sports jacket in one arm and glanced around the untidy room.

"Hi, guy," he said, not looking straight at Tom. Reichert, Tom noticed, seemed to have an aversion to doing that, just as he had an aversion to using people's names. Instead, he favoured impersonal substitutions: it was "Hi, guy!" or "Right, love!" or "Sure, pal!" as the occasion might warrant. A man in his mid-thirties or early forties — about his mother's age — he had a beer belly and wore flashy ties. Tom hated to come too close to Chuck Reichert because his aftershave smelled like insect repellent.

"We're going to have a bite to eat, then Chuck and I are going bowling," his mother told him. "I brought you a triple-cheese pizza and some Orangina. I guess you're going to a movie, are you?"

"Good way to beat the heat," Chuck called out. He had tossed his jacket on an armchair and was already in the kitchen, rattling around in the fridge in search of a beer.

"Maybe. I was at Grandpa's all afternoon and I ate a ton," Tom lied. "If you don't need me I'll go and play some pool with Pete. He just called me."

Tom had learned that white lies sounded better if you spiced them with a bit of truth. He would have loved the pizza but there was no way he was going to hang around the apartment with Chuck Reichert there. He could walk around for a while, and when they took off for bowling he'd come back and eat in peace.

"You're going to put a shirt on, I hope," his mother said. She looked at him intently, as if she was trying to read his mind — it was a look he knew, and it always made him feel uncomfortable.

"Sure."

He retreated into his room, grabbed a T-shirt from a peg, and slipped it on.

"How's Grandpa?" his mother called out. Then: "Oh, you didn't even finish the dishes!" She was already in the kitchen, tearing open parcels and shifting pots and pans. He mumbled an excuse and moved back into the living room, where Reichert had settled down with a beer. He was watching the television news and scooping handfuls of chips from a bowl.

"Mets losing again," he announced. "Why don't they get their act together?"

"See you later, Mom," Tom said. "Sorry about the cleanup." He could see her in the kitchen, busily making their dinner while Reichert flipped channels and munched.

She turned quickly and came to him. His mother was tall and slender, and she was pretty for her age, he knew. Her dark hair was stylishly cut and, as Grandpa Sandalls boasted, she had "poems instead of eyes." Tom

noticed that she looked nervous and tired, however —
her face was unusually pale and her greenish eyes dark-
circled. He couldn't understand why she would waste
her limited energy on a guy like Reichert.

She stopped in front of him and looked at him as if
she were measuring how put out he was. Then she
reached out and patted him on the shoulder.

"See you later, Tom. Don't forget your key. I won't
be late. You have a good time. We'll have a talk about
your day later."

"Is that pan out there burning?" Reichert asked.

"Why don't you get up and turn the heat down,"
Tom said.

Reichert guffawed, but his mother looked worried.
"It's all right, dear," she said. She patted his shoulder
again and retreated quickly to the kitchen.

Tom felt he was suffocating. He had started for the
door when his eye caught the *Heavy Metal* comic lying
on the floor near Reichert's stockinged feet. He ducked
back, picked up the comic without looking at Reichert,
and carried it to the door. Quickly, he slipped the envelope out, dropped the comic inside the coat closet, and
left the apartment.

He walked down the stairs, grim and close to tears.
It was sad that his mother had to hang out with guys
like Reichert. But the A&P was a "chummy place," as
she said. She was a great worrier and she seemed to be
afraid that if she wasn't sociable she'd lose her job.
Although there were other jobs around she had become
a section manager at the store and got good discounts

on the groceries. The location suited her well and she was afraid of changes.

Tom knew this, but he also knew that she had lost her confidence when his father had pulled out. Apparently the passing of time since then hadn't made much difference. He'd overheard her telling this to a friend on the phone one day. She must be lonely, he knew that, too, but he thought it was miserable to fill up the time as she did. Keeping close track of Grandpa, seeing a woman friend now and then, going out to the store parties with guys like Reichert — it wasn't much of a life.

He knew his mother was smart; she'd had two years at a community college, she took out interesting library books — not just the romances — and if she had to go out why couldn't it be with lawyers or executives? He could see her in a nice suburban house, driving her own car, and doing charity work in her spare time. Or maybe selling real estate. He thought she should make up an ad for herself and put it in the companions column of the newspaper — maybe she could find a decent man that way. Of course he was ashamed to raise the issue — the notion of his mother shopping around for a man and settling down with a stranger disturbed him. They were quite happy together, despite their lack of money, and he didn't want anything to spoil it. There were a lot of creeps out there, even worse than Reichert. If he could only work some magic and have her stay exactly as she was! He would grow older and she wouldn't, and he would earn lots of money and give her fine things while she was still young enough to enjoy them.

Tom walked slowly toward the postbox on the next corner. It was getting on toward that sunset time when the heat seemed to gather all its power. The old folks had disappeared; they were asleep or scrounging up dinner. A few unfortunate pedestrians struggled home from work, stopping to mop their brows or to exchange complaints about the weather. Cars rolled by in air-conditioned splendour. The cats had come out of the shade.

At the corner by the mailbox, Tom stopped to take a last look at the envelope. Should he drop it in the box or in the trash can?

A girl was coming toward him up Hamilton Street, a familiar figure, dressed in cotton shorts and a white T-shirt. He recognized Estella Lopez and shoved the envelope quickly in the box. He hesitated, eager to get away, although he didn't want to be rude about it.

"You look guilty," she said, as he hung there, undecided, smiling weakly in response to her two-handed wave. "What's up?"

"Just mailing a letter — for my mom."

"How's it going? I didn't see you at the Fabricon interviews."

"What's this with Fabricon? I don't need to work at Fabricon. I work at Damato's Diner."

"You might earn more at Fabricon. I'll save enough to go visit my aunt in Puerto Rico. They'll even set me up to make contact with kids down there. They give you lots of responsibility. It's a new company policy."

Estella, not very tall, was a girl who knew how to stand still and give you her attention. Her fine glossy hair was cut short; she had smooth dark skin and very dark eyes. She looked cool despite the heat, and Tom found her quietness appealing, although he didn't think she was much to look at. Still, it was nice to know that some girls were sensible and didn't always have to do a routine for you. He also knew that her father, like his, had taken off some years before and left the family. She had two brothers, which made it tough for her mother, he guessed.

"Looks like Fabricon is going to own this city soon, judging by the number of people they're hiring," Tom said. He glanced back down Morris Street, but of course it was too soon to expect his mother and Reichert to leave.

"You want to walk me over to Pitt Park?" Estella asked. "I have to meet Maggie there. You might like to see Maggie."

"I don't want to see Maggie, but I don't mind walking you." *Anything to kill time*, he thought. Anything to get them on their way. Then he could go back, eat the pizza, and watch television.

They started out, circumventing Hollis Street, instinctively taking the shortcut through the back streets of Mechanicstown. They had both lived there nearly all their lives.

"Maggie's going out for cheerleading captain next year," Estella said.

"Cheerleading sucks and so does Maggie."

Estella giggled. Maggie was a beauty and Estella just assumed he would be thrilled to see her. But he hated being "set up" like that, especially with some popular girl who was sure to scorn him.

"What do you do at Fabricon?" he asked. They were passing Swartz's Grocery and he quickened the pace a bit. He didn't particularly want to be spotted walking with Estella.

"I'm building the future," Estella said, and laughed. "You should work for them too."

"Yeah, sure. But what do they pay you for?"

"I learn how their software works, how they design it, why it's the best on the world market. I spread the word."

"You spread the word? What is it? A religion?"

"It's a good company. Pete told me they have a guy named Dr. Tarn working for them. He's a genius of computers. He thinks the human brain is just a flesh computer."

The idea sounded very cold and mechanical to Tom.

"The brain might be flesh," he said, "but the mind is something entirely different."

"Actually, Pete said that the mind is just a directory for what the brain turns out. There's no mind outside of the brain. He must have got that from Dr. Tarn."

"Isn't that unreligious?"

"Since when are you religious, Tom?"

"I'm not. I was just asking."

It was cooler in the narrow streets, but even so the air was heavy, sultry, and everything seemed drenched with moisture, leaden. Tom cursed silently that he had no change to buy them each a drink. They were taking longer than they need have because they didn't want to walk down Tweed Alley. That was where the motorcycle gangs hung out and where some kids went to buy drugs. It wasn't a great idea to go near there unless you were in the market for something.

They skirted the railroad tracks, Higgins lumber yard, and Scottsborough Public School, a wreck of decaying brick and mortar shut down long ago, boarded up and often vandalized. Some of the kids used to go there to fool around but rumours of giant rats cooled their ardour and cozier spots had been found.

Tom remembered how his father used to tell him stories about rat-infested slums that burned like brushwood, and about how he had climbed the walls of the "worst firetraps in the city." And Joe Blake had many tales about the strange things firemen came across when they investigated false alarms. His father had always been a great storyteller. He had never made himself out to be a hero, either, although he had at least one medal for bravery.

Tom wondered if his dad missed telling those stories after he ran out on the family and his mother refused ever to see him again. He knew his mother was justifiably angry, but there was a gap there, and nothing, or no one, had come along to fill it.

After a while they came out onto a street of low apartment buildings, weathered brick structures with brass plates around the doorways, transoms, and quaint names, like The Victoria, The Foxgrove, The Sherwood. Tom could see the tall poplars, the old maples of Pitt Park, and the dome of the ancient bathhouse rising above the hedges and the iron fences.

It's time to turn back, he thought. The chip wagon near the entrance was where the kids hung out and he didn't want to show up with Estella — they might start kidding him about being sweet on her. He told her he should be taking off.

"At least get a drink before you cut out," she suggested. "You'll collapse from dehydration otherwise."

He shrugged. The drinking fountain was in a small square that enclosed a mini playground and allowed entrance to one end of the park. They weren't likely to meet anyone there. There was no sign of the beautiful Maggie, either.

They crossed the street. The smell of shrubbery was pleasant, the air much cooler.

The square was only fifty yards further on. They turned in and saw a mother swinging a child, some children playing ball, two old men on a bench mulling over their chess moves. On another bench a figure was lying hunched up — it was a guy wearing only shorts and a T-shirt and looking like he was bushed or asleep or pretty drunk. Tom was surprised — layabouts weren't a usual sight in the park because the police didn't tolerate them. There was a lot of civic pride in West Hope's boast that all its parks and playgrounds were safe.

"I'm dying of thirst," Estella said.

"Too bad I don't have any money," Tom explained.

"The water fountain is just fine."

The water rose and trickled in the stone basin, one of those things that had been there forever, it seemed.

They drank in turn and Tom splashed his face and arms with the water. It felt good. Children shouted and ran past. He drank more, and, still bent over, caught a glimpse of the figure stretched on the bench. Something caught his attention. The sleeper swung his arms away from his head and Tom saw to his astonishment that it was Jeff Parker.

"Jeez, look! It's Jeff."

Estella took a step toward the park bench where he pointed. "He doesn't look good — and you know how he runs. Maybe it's heat exhaustion. Let's check it out!"

They walked hurriedly past the shouting children. As they approached the bench Jeff swung his body up, letting his legs dangle down. He looked relaxed, and as they came nearer he smiled.

"You OK, Jeff?" Tom said. "We saw you lying there like a corpse."

"Hey, I' m not dead yet, man. I've just seen the light, that's all. Can't stay in motion the whole time. Got to use the head computer too, you know."

Tom stopped in his tracks. There was a lazy swing to his sentences that made it sound like anyone but Jeff. His eyes seemed to have a slight glaze. He must have been smoking pot, Tom decided — but Jeff? He just didn't do the stuff. And what was this talk about a head computer? This didn't sound like Jeff at all!

"Are you sure you're OK?" Tom asked.

"Sure am, Little Red Riding Hood. How was Grandpa doing?"

"Fine."

"I saw you running earlier," Estella said. "How did it go?"

"It went just fine. I ran into Pete Halloran. Pete offered to run with me too, but I didn't think he could stick it in this heat. Then he took me over to Fabricon. He introduced me to some cool people there. What a place!"

"It's the wave of the future," Estella said. "Everybody wants to work for Fabricon."

"I wish you'd told me about it sooner," Jeff said. "I'm going to do some promoting for them. It means giving up a bit of running time, but hell, man, the money's terrific and it's my future I have to think of."

"Are you crazy? You've already got a great future. What about all those scholarships?" Tom could hardly contain himself. "Is everybody crazy? This Fabricon's turning the town upside down. It's like an infection!"

Jeff looked at Estella and smiled. "What's with this guy, anyway? Don't he know where it's at? Why don't you take him over there, baby? He should see this oper-ation with his own eyes."

Estella nodded and reached out for Tom. "You should come with us." It was as if she wanted to lead him straight to Fabricon. He shook his head and backed off quickly.

"Sorry, I've got to go now!" Tom looked from one to the other, stunned by their odd expressions, their knowing glances. It was as if they shared a secret that he was denied — and he didn't like it.

"See you soon!" he shouted and began to jog back toward the park gate. Their shouted greetings trailed after him, but he didn't turn around.

He moved quickly past the old men at their chess game on the bench, past the screaming children. He ducked around a young woman walking a spaniel. He could feel his body, tense and a little tired, begin to relax. The sunlight on the trees was dazzling. The traffic up ahead had thinned out. Just another evening in the city.

Normal! Everything as usual! And yet something wasn't quite right. There was too much of Fabricon in the air and in the heads of his friends. What could it mean? He ran, hoping that when he got there the apartment would be empty. He needed time to be alone, to think. To figure out what was going on in West Hope — and whether the problem was his or everybody else's.

CHAPTER THREE

The Shadow Knows

Tom returned home to find the apartment empty. For a while he sat aimlessly in the heat, staring at the walls, peering out the window. He ate the pizza and drank gallons of water, all the time wondering whether there was something really wrong with this Fabricon business or whether he was just imagining a lot of crazy things. Nothing much happened in West Hope; all the kids were planning to make it somewhere else, just serving time until they could escape the place. Meanwhile, why not latch onto something good, why not take a job where the action was?

Maybe it was the same old story. Maybe his friends were just smart and he was the one who was slow off the mark, the one who held back. He felt suddenly left out and miserable, but at the same time grimly determined. He would make it, despite the odds. He would get out of this apartment, out of this city. Yet right now he couldn't think of what to do. He didn't really have anyone to confide in.

He took one last look out the window. It was dark and not much cooler. Voices sounded from the pavement below, a fire engine whined in the distance. He wondered if his mother was having a good time. How could she, with a guy like Reichert?

A terrible thought struck him then. Suppose his mother really liked Reichert? Suppose she even married him? They would settle down and she would be stuck forever at the supermarket. Or she would have another child — Reichert's child — and he would have to leave — but then with Reichert hanging around, he would have to leave anyway.

Tom couldn't bear to think about that possibility any longer. He turned on the television and flipped through the channels. There was nothing to settle on, so he surfed endlessly up and down, the remote clutched in his right hand, a magic wand without any magic.

He felt guilty as he did so. "Why don't you read a book sometime," his mother would say. "You watch too much television. You're becoming a couch potato and you'll end up like Paddy Watson." (Paddy Watson, a high school friend of Tom's mother's, had grown fat watching television. He did nothing else. It was television and junk food all the way. "Vicarious living," Tom's mother called it. "You're there but you're not there." But Paddy had suffered a heart attack and was having to make a few feeble efforts now to get his body in motion, to get off the couch and do something.)

After a while Tom got tired and went to bed. As he lay in the dark his body, his soul, seemed to cry out for something. But he wasn't listening. He was listening for his mother's footsteps in the hall, her key in the lock.

Later, half-swamped by crazy dreams, he heard voices, whispers, but he was too tired to get up. Then suddenly there was light, a show of dawn at the window. He lay waiting for his mother's alarm to go off. It did and he heard her stirring about, coughing, then water running and the kitchen radio at low volume. He knew she would be coming in to say goodbye to him and he steeled himself.

"Did you have a good time?" he growled, as she bent over the bed to kiss him goodbye.

"It was fun," she told him, her voice cool and contained. "But I'm sorry you and I didn't have a chance to talk."

He didn't say anything. Her perfume seemed to hover in the stuffy air. He pulled the covers more tightly around his body and waited. A few minutes passed. Noises in the kitchen and living room. It sounded as if she might be going.

"Have a good day," he called out.

"You too, darling."

When he heard the door shut he dragged himself up and struggled to the window, wiping the sleep out of his eyes at every step. He watched her walk down toward Hollis Street, then he went to the bathroom, splashed some cold water in his face, fetched a bottle of cold orange juice from the fridge, and nearly emptied it.

He made himself an omelette — it was something he did well — and ate it while he flipped the television channels. He stopped at a show that was featuring famous comic book and pulp heroes and villains. Some smart-assed professor guy was talking about The Shadow, Lamont Cranston, "who clouds men's minds so that they cannot see him." The professor only had thirty seconds or so to make his point, but he did it pretty well.

"The Shadow is a symbolic figure," he said. "He understands evil and can deal with it because he's part of it. He acknowledges his own capacity for crime. He walks on the dark side to find the light. The villains can't see him because he looks too much like them. He's really their dark side turning against them."

End of clip. Tom stood up and flipped off the television. The apartment was penetrated by sunlight, and the hot hazy day was beginning to suffocate the city, but Tom suddenly had a plan, one that involved darkness, shadows, and the night.

He felt excited, on the edge, but confident. He would spend the day getting ready and then he would do some exploring.

He went out and bought some small drink packs, a few snacks, and batteries for his pocket flashlight. He spent some time looking at the city map. He knew the streets and byways very well already, but there was no harm in refreshing your memory.

He called Pete to see if he wanted to play pool, but his mother said he had gone to work at Fabricon. Tom went to the video store and picked up a couple of John

Woo movies and spent the day watching them. By the time he took them back, had a sleep, and tidied up the apartment, it was getting on time for his mother to arrive.

He sat down and wrote her a note, telling her he had gone to play pool and that he might go to a movie after, but he wouldn't be very late.

He had found an old belt-clip into which he stuffed a drink box, some crackers and cheese, the flashlight, a small notepad, and a pen. He locked the door, pocketed the key, and got out of the building as quickly as possible. His mother occasionally got off early and he wasn't taking any chances.

He had to kill some time until nearly sunset, so he went down to the branch library and looked up old maps of the city. Sure enough, he found one showing the amusement park, as well as the milk bottling plant that had been torn down when Fabricon built its new headquarters. He also found some newspaper files that explained why the computer firm had not taken the usual route and located in the suburbs. The city, pushing for new development, had offered them significant benefits to move into the run-down river area. The story was accompanied by a picture of the mayor shaking hands with the company CEO, Dr. Martin J. Binkley, a handsome, youngish man, well dressed and seemingly at ease, smiling at the camera.

Another figure in the photo caught Tom's attention. Just to the left of Binkley he saw a short, round, bald-headed older man dressed in a plaid jacket and facing the camera with an expression that lay somewhere between disdain and suppressed amusement. The caption identified the man as Dr. Willis Tarn, head of Fabricon's Research Division.

Tom had checked out the company's Web page, a glossy site that emphasized Fabricon's economic importance for West Hope and its boast that "Progress is our biggest priority." There were pictures of impressive laboratories, clean-cut young scientists, and space vehicles, and quotations from Newton and Einstein.

Yet Tom remembered some of the things he had read or heard about Dr. Tarn — that he was a research genius and a disciple of the greatest of the MIT computer gurus. That he was a fast liver who liked expensive houses and cars and the company of beautiful young women. That he had predicted that religion and spirituality would soon vanish from society, to be replaced by the brotherhood of the Web.

Dr. Tarn was known as a man who didn't mince words. In an exchange with a local Episcopalian minister he suggested that the minister's warnings about technology were the result of "insufficient brain wiring" and he offered to fix the problem in his laboratory. He suggested to the local Social Welfare Council that the only way to cure poverty was to eliminate the unfit. This would be done, he explained, once genetic engineering had been perfected. Dr. Tarn claimed that Fabricon was about to put West Hope on the map, and he was constantly denying rumours that the firm would relocate to California, Carolina, or Mexico as soon as it reached a certain sales volume.

Tom didn't like the sound of Dr. Tarn at all and wondered how Fabricon could be so popular with a man like that behind it. He was glad to put the files away and to escape into the streets, even though the heat made him catch his breath and soon slowed his steps to a slow walk.

He knew exactly where he was going, though.

Avoiding Morris and Hollis and the whole main drag, he headed north toward the river, choosing the back streets of Mechanicstown, picking his way through the old Italian section (which was now mostly Vietnamese), past Precious Blood Church, scene of the funeral of one of his friends, past the Beth-Israel Synagogue and the shooting gallery, then into a maze of several blocks of rundown warehouses, which the kids called Rat City.

This was a locked-in, suffocating part of town, and since most of the businesses had shut down long ago the streets were almost deserted. He and Pete had walked over this way a few times and he knew that if he just kept a wary eye on the alleys and the cars cruising by, if he moved along quickly without seeming to notice anybody or anything, he would be OK.

After walking a few blocks past the boarded-up wrecks of buildings, crumbling facades with blank windows and graffiti-smeared walls, he reached the ancient wreck of the railway station and saw it was nearly time to turn west. Here the polluted river flowed into an old basin where barges must have once moored.

Gulls flapped and shrieked above the stinking water, above the ruins of the storage depots, deserted truck havens, and abandoned warehouses. The old railway line had been nearly choked by foul undergrowth, and the tracks ran along between the spikes of an iron fence, amid a riot of rambling bush, spindly trees, and poison ivy. A huge rusty crane sat near a row of shacks, a ghoulish monument, and the way ahead was littered with paper and bits of old tires. Even the street signs were bent and battered, as if someone had taken his revenge on them for having to find his way through such a place.

Still, it was a good way to go — he wasn't likely to meet any of the gang here. And sure enough, as he approached River Street with its weathered row houses and apartment buildings, he came on a different scene: a few old men walking dogs, women chatting in small backyards, little kids playing handball. When he passed one or two corner stores with outside fruit stands and newspaper racks, he knew that the worst of the walk was over.

He had timed it perfectly, too, since the light was fading and darkness was beginning to take over the cavernous streets.

Now he had a wide view of things. He could see the river, snakelike and sombre, as it turned away to the north, its three iron bridges sinking into shadow, its barges heaped with scrap and garbage. Warehouses ran along the bottom of Harbour Street beside the jetty. Beyond the main thoroughfare lay the amusement park, a grim Xanadu with spearlike gates and fence, an onion-domed main building, and the remains of an old roller coaster with a car immobilized on the top of the run, as if time had stopped in the middle of the last ride.

The place had been closed for years now, but Tom vaguely remembered being taken there as a kid. He had been afraid of the roller coaster but intrigued by the funhouse, which included distorting mirrors, skewed floors that made one stagger, dark passages echoing with eerie voices, figures that appeared and disappeared as mysterious doors opened and closed.

That was a lost world, but what about Mercury House? Tom walked a little farther up the street and found number 221 Harbour — an old clapboard building, ramshackle and neglected, flanked on either side by grimy sheds. It looked, as his grandfather had said, as if any day now the city would step in and tear it down.

Embarrassed at having sent a letter to such a place and wishing now that he could take it back, Tom continued up the street. Mercury Man had vanished forever; he was gone with the old days and the old dreams — and it was no good pretending otherwise.

Farther up Harbour Street another sight undermined his confidence and almost made him doubt the whole point of his night's mission. He saw a tall white building, sleek and modern, its windows gleaming with the poetry of the fading sunlight. Fabricon. The place was impressive, clean, and modern, classically simple and reassuring. And, by all accounts, wonderful discoveries were taking place inside. Emblazoned across two sides of the building near the top were two big signs, illuminated every night. "FABRICON INC." the topmost one announced, and just below it, in slightly smaller letters the second advised: "READ THE FUTURE IN US."

Was it really likely that anything weird could be happening in such an efficient and clean-lined setting? The building shone like a white beacon and its many windows seemed to insist that this was a place with nothing to hide.

Tom gritted his teeth and decided that, whatever his doubts, he had to go through with his plan. The idea of a Mercury Man ring and a porthole might be a bit dumb, but he knew what he'd seen with his own eyes. The kids had been acting strangely. There was too much sudden enthusiasm for Fabricon. No harm in checking things out.

He knew that just opposite the computer firm, along Harbour Street, there were several renovated office buildings that had sprung up in the wake of the new development. Behind them, running parallel to Harbour, lay Water Lane, and Tom figured he could approach the building by that route. All he had to do then was hang out in the little park opposite Fabricon. From there he could size the place up and get a sense of anything weird that might be going on.

He turned and made his way back to Water Lane. It was a narrow but relatively prosperous thoroughfare, with lawyer's offices, architecture firms, trading companies, and other professional outfits occupying the brownstones that had miraculously survived the many changes in this area of town.

Tom kept a steady pace, taking note of the houses with their added-on studios, their clever landscaping, the parked BMWs, and the well-dressed men and women who materialized in the doorways. They had worked late, he supposed, and were anxious to be getting home. They all looked so clean and cool — everything was air-conditioned here — while Tom, drenched in sweat, felt dirty and out of place. He was sure that, if anyone had noticed, they would have found his clothes pathetic, the belt-clip ridiculous, and the whole idea of a sinister Fabricon absurd.

"Get yourself a life, kid," they would have said, which in a way was what everyone was telling him.

He walked on, and after a while he turned west to get to Harbour. He found the park, an open space with a fountain and trees, a few benches, washrooms, and a bus stop shelter. Occasionally a fish and chips or sausage vendor would set up there, but at that moment it was deserted. Tom breathed a sigh of relief. It should be the perfect place from which to keep an eye on Fabricon.

Tom stood in the darkness between a beech tree and some withered bushes and gazed across at the front entrance of the computer firm. A pity he couldn't have brought Grandpa's binoculars, but he'd been afraid they would attract attention.

Luckily, his eyesight was good and he had a direct view of the place.

The brass door, beneath the elegant awning, shone now like a polished shield. From his brief spring visit, Tom remembered what was behind it. He pictured the huge hall with its tiled floor, its walls hung with historic scenes of West Hope. He remembered the small brass fountain discreetly set off by potted cactus plants, a display case illustrating "Fabulous Fabricon" (this included pictures of successful personnel, trophies, plaques, and the like), and, somewhat to the rear of the fountain, a security desk that barred entrance to all but the invited. Tom and Pete, however, had actually made it to a waiting room before being politely but firmly kicked out.

Tom watched intently for a while, but little was happening across the way. It was 8:25, well past dinnertime, and the evening shifts might be working. He munched on a sandwich, wondering what his mother had thought of his note and whether she would be going out with Reichert again. The image of that slouching sleazebag made him want to spit. Instead, he sipped some juice and waited.

His patience was rewarded some minutes later when an expensive-looking sleek blue convertible pulled up at the Fabricon entrance. The driver, a balding, stocky figure in a white summer shirt and slacks, jumped from the car, and Tom recognized him at once.

Dr. Tarn stood for a moment, staring across Harbour Street (Tom almost felt that the man was looking right at him and shrank back). Then the passenger, a slim young blonde in a halter top, slid across and took over the wheel. Tarn bent to kiss her briefly, and even from where he stood Tom could hear her tinkling laughter.

Tarn turned quickly, swinging a small black briefcase, and disappeared into the building. Tom took out his notebook and wrote down the time. But what to do now? He couldn't follow Tarn inside. Was he going to wait the whole night and note down who came and went?

The next minutes passed rather slowly. Then, just as he was beginning to lose patience, something else happened.

A red company van cruised slowly down Harbour Street and drew up at the door where a few minutes before the Mercedes had deposited Tarn.

The van seemed crowded with passengers, shifting and stirring behind the glass. When they began to scramble out, Tom craned his neck to see them, but the vehicle obstructed his view. "Move that thing," he whispered. "Move it, you stupid idiot!"

The van didn't move for some minutes, but luckily the passengers were in no hurry to get out and enter the building. Tom could hear their voices as they laughed and joked around and he could see them pushing and shoving together at the vehicle's doors and on the sidewalk. *Kids*, he thought, *a bunch of high school kids.*

Finally, amid shouts and cheers, the van emptied; slowly it pulled away and the passengers stood at last in full view. With a gasp Tom recognized Bim, Pete, Estella, and Jeff Parker.

He was surprised at the feelings that overcame him then. He saw his friends joking and laughing together on the sidewalk, not very far away, and yet they seemed like total strangers. He felt completely alone, isolated, left out, and deceived. On the one hand he had a great desire to be with them — and after all, they had invited him! On the other hand he didn't want any part of it. He wanted to get away right now, to hide out somewhere and be strong and single and solitary in his aloneness. The worst thing would be if they noticed him hiding here like a fool. God! How they'd laugh at him!

Slowly, much too slowly, the bad moments passed. The kids began to drift inside. Within minutes the entrance to Fabricon was once again surrounded by a shrinelike silence.

Tom gritted his teeth. He had to think. He had to figure things out.

What in hell was going on?

Why had they suddenly arrived like that? He knew the kids couldn't all be on one shift. Jeff and Bim didn't even have jobs there yet. Were they all going to some kind of training meeting? An indoctrination? *What kind of indoctrination?*

Was he making too much of things because he himself didn't have the guts to take on a challenge? Reluctantly, he admitted it might be so. *But what did Fabricon want with the kids?*

Tom stood in perplexity, staring at the towering, perfect building opposite. Fabricon's white facade suggested the beautiful sterility of a gigantic laboratory; its gleaming glass indicated openness and transparency of purpose; its emblazoned slogan promised miracles for the future. His friends might be caught up in something, yet they were no fools. Maybe if he just had a few quiet words with them …

Tom mopped his sweating forehead, wiped his hands on his cut-off jeans, and moved slowly out of the trees and toward one of the benches. Deeply preoccupied, he had lost all sense of his surroundings. He turned to survey the streets and the little park, as if he might find the answer there.

It was then that he saw the figure in the shadows. A tall man in a black running suit, standing and glaring at him with a fierce and particular intensity.

Tom stepped back. The man came forward.

"You!" he shouted.

For an instant Tom stood frozen, then he turned and ran, at top speed, in the direction of Fabricon.

CHAPTER FOUR

Inside the Future

Tom ran blindly, straight into Harbour Street. A taxi swerved and missed him, its horn blaring. He caught a glimpse of the driver's face, startled and angry together, but the cab went on without stopping.

A car came the other way and the woman who was driving, taking no chances, leaned on her horn, then slowed down and shook her finger in Tom's direction. He thought he recognized her as one of last year's teachers and ducked away.

He hustled out of the street and straight up to Fabricon's entrance.

His heart was pounding; his breath came in gasps. His hands touched the cold metal of the company door.

The man in black had not followed him across. He had remained in front of the park, jogging around, pretending to read the bus schedule.

He was clever, acting as if he were just killing time, but Tom wasn't fooled. He knew the man was watching him.

Is he trying to scare me away, to drive me inside the building? Tom took a deep breath. *Or is he just some weirdo hanging around parks? There's got to be a way of figuring this out.*

Into his mind suddenly came the image of his friends, scrambling out of the van and into Fabricon. They had seemed happy enough; they weren't being kidnapped. And yet it was odd that they were all there together, trooping dutifully into Fabricon as if they were following some Pied Piper. Something was going on — he was sure of it. There had to be a way to find them, to figure things out for himself, to get his own take on Fabricon.

At that moment two men appeared in the hall inside. They had materialized from a nearby corridor and were laughing and talking, reaching for cigarettes as they moved.

They came straight out the door and Tom stepped aside to let them pass. They ignored him, absorbed in conversation.

"What did she say then?" one of the men asked.

"You won't believe this, but she told me she liked the new program."

They lit cigarettes and walked south up Harbour. The man in the park was no longer visible, but Tom could almost sense his presence.

He knew that as soon as he moved, as soon as he started to head back to the safety of home or his grandfather's place, the man would be after him.

He stepped boldly through the door and into the great hall of Fabricon.

It was exactly as he remembered it, and he quickly circumnavigated the fountain and headed straight for the guard desk.

A grizzled old man looked up from his tabloid paper.

"What can I do for you?" he asked, keeping most of his attention on the paper.

"I hope I'm not too late," Tom said. He tried — it wasn't difficult — to sound breathless and eager. "I missed the pickup and I guess the kids are already here. I ran after the red van but I just missed it."

"Oh, *them* kids. Sure. And what would your name be?"

"Bim Bavasi," Tom said. His own name, he knew, wouldn't be on any list.

"Just a minute, I'll call up and tell them."

Now Tom was desperate. They would know that Bim was already there; he would be exposed at once.

"Excuse me, sir," he said, as the man started dialling. "Is there a men's room here I could use?"

"Right through them doors, kid. And don't disappear — they'll be sending someone down in a minute."

Tom stepped quickly through the doors and into the inner sanctum. Luckily, he had remembered from his spring visit that there was a restroom there. He had no intention of stopping there now, however.

As soon as he was out of the watchman's sight, he sprinted away down the corridor.

He turned a corner and came upon an even longer corridor — a softly lit, restful space, it was lined with blue doors and decorated with abstract paintings that looked like spreadsheet graphs. Inscriptions on the doors bore the names of famous scientists: Einstein, Planck, Darwin, and others. There was nothing else in the hall except a fancy looking water cooler.

It looked as if he had hustled his way into a dead end, and he was tempted by the red exit sign at the far end. But it was just an emergency door: he had boxed himself in. They would soon be after him and he would be exposed and humiliated. Was that what his pursuer had wanted? Or was he waiting outside for the inevitable conclusion?

Tom stopped. He had no idea what to do.

The door marked "Einstein" opened, and a woman in a white lab jacket stepped out. She looked at him casually, then more sharply.

"Can I help you?" She was noticing his rough clothes and probably his panic.

"Yeah. My friends came over in a red van. I missed it, so I came on my bike. There was nobody out there to ask, so I thought I'd just look for them myself."

The woman's expression lightened.

"Good old Mac was out for a smoke, was he? I think I know what you want. That's the Fabricon Youth Group. There's a stairway there, right next to Darwin, you see? The Youth Group meets on the second floor. In the auditorium, usually — it's called Copernicus Hall. You can't miss it."

"Thanks a lot, ma'am."

Tom smiled and, restraining himself, found the stairwell. Once out of sight, he turned on all the jets, bounded up two steps at a time, pushed through another door, and emerged in a larger, more imposing space.

It was huge, as big as a basketball court, but its smooth white walls were lined with display cases, while its arched ceiling made him think of a church. At the far end, high up, hung a metallic robot the size of a small car, dangling on invisible wires above some cushioned chairs and couches. A couple of men sat there, tiny figures beneath the robot, their backs to where Tom stood. They seemed reposeful enough, until a third man appeared from somewhere and said, in a voice loud enough for Tom to hear, "There's a kid roaming around here, looking for his pals. They're all with Tarn now in Copernicus and he doesn't want to be disturbed. If you run into this kid have him wait right here until Tarn gets through with them."

One of the men said something in reply. Tom, who had crouched down behind a display case, couldn't hear it, but he heard their laughter. When he dared to look again, the third man had disappeared and the first two men were sitting placidly together.

If he were caught, the great Dr. Tarn would speak to him. That was a possibility he didn't exactly look forward to.

Examining the hall more carefully now he saw that it was rimmed, several levels higher, by a kind of balcony — a narrow walkway such as sometimes gives access to the higher shelves in old libraries. He saw, too, that about twenty feet away there was a curved metal staircase by which he could reach this walkway. Once up there, he might be able to get a look into Copernicus

Hall without being seen. The only trouble was that to do so he would have to walk out in full view of anyone who might come out of any of the many doors that lined both the upper and lower levels of the place.

The situation seemed hopeless, but then he noticed, a few feet away, a numbered door that looked like it might be a maintenance closet. This gave him an idea, and he crept slowly and carefully forward, keeping his eye on the two men down the hall, hopeful that they wouldn't turn and spot him.

He reached the closet, turned the handle, and found that it was open. He was inside in an instant, and he pulled the door shut behind him and flipped on the light. Sure enough, there was a small washbasin, a few mops, brooms, and pails, and the smell of soap and disinfectant.

When he saw the rough bundled clothing hung on metal pegs in one corner, he sprang forward. He was in luck! Here he had a ready-made disguise that might just do the trick.

Quickly, he pulled on the work overalls — they were a little small but he managed to get into them. There was even a cap, which he tore at to make it fit his head. He gawked at himself in the mirror, laughed, and grabbed a pail and mop.

He took a deep breath, slowly opened the door, and stepped back into the corridor.

He walked forward without much confidence. He knew that, above all, he had to look bored and casual. Workmen didn't stalk around places holding mops like swords or lances. Deliberately, as he climbed the curving stairway, he clattered the pail against the metal banister. The men in the lounge area turned at once, threw him a glance, then paid him no further attention.

He took a deep breath. He had passed the first test. Up the stairs he climbed, until he emerged on the narrow walkway, high above the main hall. He stopped for a minute, pretending to work at a patch of floor. He had to move forward along the balcony to reach the auditorium.

He went slowly and carefully, and his confidence built up a little. It looked like he just might make it. Then suddenly a door opened right behind him and voices sounded so close in his ear that he jumped and gasped. He had sense enough, though, not to spring around, to keep on mopping. His heart pounded wildly as a man and a woman stepped around him, negotiating the narrow space together.

"Evening," he mumbled in his deepest voice, without daring to look at them.

"Evening," the woman replied.

They walked on past, engrossed in their conversation, and disappeared into another room. He picked up his mop and continued, as deliberately as he could, in the direction of the auditorium. A man walked out of a room just in front of him.

Tom turned quickly, set the pail and mop aside, pulled a rag out of his pocket, and pretended to polish the tiled wall. The man walked past without a word.

Despite its lofty spaces, the main Fabricon hall seemed claustrophobic. He resumed his march forward, but anxious thoughts assailed him. Suppose they caught him? He wanted to find out where his friends were, but what about the risks? He could be arrested for trespassing, or even worse. In which case his mother would be frantic.

A few anxious moments later he had reached a point just opposite the robot figure that dominated the lofty hall. Close up he could see that it was really a comical sculpture, a jolly construction suspended from on high by invisible wires. It looked like a composite of all the robots he had seen in science fiction movies, and it had some kind of formula (or was it a secret language?) written across its metallic chest. Underneath it, far below, sat the two men he had spotted earlier, still busy with their coffee, magazines, and casual conversation.

Tom hesitated a moment. The men, chatting together, seemed oblivious to his presence. A few steps farther, then, on the right, almost at his elbow, he saw large double doors fixed with a brass plate that bore the inscription "COPERNICUS." Underneath this, a sheet of paper had been pinned up. It read: "Experiment in Progress. Absolutely no admittance."

He hesitated, hearing faint noises from within, but moved on toward where the walkway curved beneath an enormous skylight. Here he came upon another, much smaller, door, this one marked "CONTROL ROOM."

He peered through a tiny window and saw, inside a dimly lit booth, elaborate machinery and a man standing behind a complicated-looking projector. The man, engrossed in his task, didn't see him, and Tom ducked back, thinking, *A movie, some kind of promo. Is this where they all are? But why the secrecy?*

There was only one way to find out. He slipped back to the entrance door, carefully removed the posted warning, and shoved it into the pocket of his overalls. He pushed gently at the door. It yielded, and there was a moment's glare of light, accompanied by a blare of sound. He stepped forward and suddenly found himself standing in the darkness of some kind of large upper chamber.

He stood there, shrinking into the shadows, waiting for a sign that his entry had been noticed. Nothing happened and he breathed easier.

A show was in progress. A seductive female voice was talking about Fabricon.

"YOU ARE PART OF THIS NOW. ALWAYS REMEMBER THAT THE FUTURE OF FABRICON IS UP TO YOU."

The voice irritated him. Beyond shadowy rows of seats and a curving line of wall, he saw a kind of chasm. The chasm seemed to be boiling up with light and sound.

The glass booth at the rear issued beams of light — a projector in action.

He was standing in a darkened balcony of Copernicus Hall and a show was in progress. "YOU ARE THE FUTURE AND THE FUTURE IS YOU," the voice said. "REPEAT WITH ME NOW. LET THE WORD RUN OVER YOUR TONGUES. FABRICON."

From the chasm, collective youthful voices chanted, "FABRICON."

Tom scrambled over the seats and peered down into the auditorium. The seats were full of faces, the darkness alive with disembodied heads. Tom was certain he could see his friends there — Bim and Pete and Estella and Jeff. They sat in rapt attention, with many others, staring up, their eyes reflecting the screen's flashing light. Held rigid, their heads seemed barely to move and their lips opened together as they chanted the single word: "FABRICON!"

Tom stood back in horror. The screen showed geometric patterns, shifting, changing, moving. He stared at them for a minute and felt his attention fixed and narrowed. It was disturbing. He could hardly tear his glance away.

What was going on down there? A training session? It seemed more than that. An indoctrination? But that smooth voice, those rhythmical lights, the chanting voices.

Was it possible? His friends were being hypnotized by Fabricon!

Even as this thought come into Tom's mind the balcony door swung open. A beam of light swept the darkness, caught him and held him. He blinked and lifted a hand to shield his eyes.

"Don't move! You! Stand right there!"

The harsh, hoarse whisper of the man in the doorway. Tom wanted to run, but before he could move, another man appeared, sprang up the aisle with lightning speed, and grabbed him roughly by the shoulder.

"C'mon you! What in hell are you doing in here?"

The second man shoved him toward the lighted doorway, while the other man, the one who had first challenged him, kept the light in his face.

"Bring him right out here," he said. "Tarn will raise hell if he finds out we've breached security."

Tom found himself out on the walkway, shoved against the wall, his captors, two clean-cut young men in white lab jackets, glaring at him, inspecting him from head to toe.

"Don't you know you're not supposed to clean in there? Didn't you read the sign?" the first man said.

"The sign's gone, Larry. Some idiot took the sign down."

The second man waved a hand in front of his eyes — Tom didn't flinch. He felt a moment of exultation. They thought he was one of the cleaning staff! That gave him an idea, a desperate idea, one that might just save him. He stared straight ahead, tried to glaze his glance, and whispered, "FABRICON. FABRICON IS THE FUTURE."

There was a pause. He sensed the puzzlement of the two men, their hesitation, but he kept his look glazed, straight ahead.

"Can you beat that!" one of the men said. "This kid's been zombied by the program. He must have wandered in there by mistake. What a mess! We'll have to get in touch with Tarn himself."

"Let's take him downstairs and lock him up. Tarn can decide what to do with him. I wonder who the hell took the sign down?"

"One of us has to stay here. Why don't you take him down? And find out who he is so we can check his records. Tarn will want to see those before he does anything. Imagine, getting accidentally zombied by the program!"

"What's going on up there?" a voice called from below. Tom knew it must be one of the men in the lower hall, but he kept his eyes fixed, his face blank.

One of the white-coated men leaned over the balcony.

"It's all right," he shouted down. "One of the cleaners had a dizzy spell. We're taking him for a little first aid."

Quickly, the other man steered Tom toward a nearby stairwell. He was avoiding the open stairs, and it was clear that the men who had shouted up knew nothing of what was happening in the projection room. A special indoctrination? A secret operation within Fabricon? That was an important fact to remember.

"What's your name, son?" the man asked as he ushered him down the stairs.

"Tom Strong," he said, making his voice as hollow as he could. It was the first name that had come into his head — the name of Mercury Man's sidekick. But there was no hero to save him now.

"You just relax and keep on walking. You've had a little episode and I'm taking you to a place where you can rest."

They came out in the corridor where Tom had begun his search. A woman in a grey suit was standing at the water fountain next to the door marked "EINSTEIN." He wasn't sure if it was the same woman who had accosted him earlier.

"So you've caught him?" she said. "Why is he dressed up like a cleaner?"

His captor pulled up short. Tom felt a rough hand on his shoulder.

"What do you mean? Caught who?" the man asked.

"Some kid got by Mac — claimed he was looking for his friends. He's probably a thief looking for some equipment."

With all his strength Tom yanked free. He stumbled once, then burst away down the corridor.

Behind him, the man swore, and the woman cried out, "Help!"

He reached the exit door. The sign read, "EMER-GENCY ONLY. NO WAY OUT."

Tom launched himself at the doors; they burst open. An alarm sounded. He was suddenly outside.

The man was after him, coming out of the lighted building. He wasn't in good shape, Tom saw, and was already breathing hard. Tom dodged around a couple of cars and sprinted across an open space. The man was still behind him, but losing ground.

Ahead was a low stone wall, and behind that the trees and bushes of Fabricon Park. Tom knew the park — there were good places to hide there — and beyond lay the city streets.

Over his shoulder Tom saw car lights go on in the parking lot. They were using a vehicle. He stopped in his tracks, tore off the cleaner's suit, and threw it away.

He sprinted toward the brightly lit park entrance, for him an open sesame into a deserted street. He had to get out of there and into the heart of the city before they cut him off. Out of the corner of his eye he could see a car coming out of the Fabricon lot. He burst through the park entrance, dashed across the street and into one of the narrow alleys that ran along the west side of Harbour Street.

He knew he still wasn't safe and was tempted to hide out for a while in the all-night grocery he found on the corner. He decided it was too risky; they might just stop and ask about him.

He ran past the grocery and found another street, one he didn't know at all. It seemed to run south toward the city, and far up ahead he could see more lights and hear the roar of real traffic. The sooner he got to a busy section, the better.

Two blocks more and he had to slow down. He was beginning to feel safer now. No sign of the car, which may have turned the wrong way or simply gone back to Fabricon.

He walked as fast as he could, looking behind him from time to time, trying to take in what had happened. He was scared and shaken up. All of a sudden he had a secret. He was a hunted kid. He was in danger.

Around him it was quiet, however, and he began to relax. When a car appeared he ducked close to a building and waited. At one point he went into a candy store and bought a Coke. He drank it near the entrance, looking up and down and watching the traffic for a while.

When he was sure he was clear of them, he walked out into the street.

A main intersection lay ahead. From there he could get to Hollis. His object was to reach home as quickly as possible. After that, he could sit down and think things out.

"No problem," he kept repeating, saying it over and over to calm himself. His legs were beginning to feel weary, leaden. He felt filthy and drenched in sweat. *No problem.*

But when he reached the next corner and pushed on toward Hollis, confident that he was free of trouble at last, he saw that there was a problem.

A tall man in a black jogging suit was trotting after him.

CHAPTER FIVE

The Pursuit Begins

For the first time, Tom was really afraid. He was gut-scared, and the fear made his tired legs seem even heavier and his shoulders sag. A kind of hopelessness crept over him and made it difficult to breathe.

I've got to keep running, he told himself. *I've got to figure this out.*

Sometimes fear brings insight. Tom was terrified, and he had no confidence he could outrun the man. But as he picked up his own speed — driving his tired body forward until it hurt — he was charting the territory just ahead of him, remembering the streets and the back alleys, trying to work out a way to escape the man's relentless pursuit.

He had already decided that he wouldn't make for home. His mother would surely be there. He might put her in danger — at the least she would be frightened and ask a lot of questions. She might even call the company.

No, he had to head for Grandpa's place. Even though he was a little afraid to face him, he knew that old Jack wouldn't panic, that he would know what to do. Tom desperately needed a plan of action.

He reached Jefferson Street and stopped on the corner. The old Y, a gloomy pile of smoke-darkened brick, stood just opposite. He stared longingly at its fortress-like bulk and at the tangled traffic up on Hollis, just one block away. Was it better to duck into a building or to stay outside? Maybe the street was safer — the man wasn't going to hurt him or grab him there. Or was he?

A police car cruised up slowly and stopped near the corner, just outside the Y. Tom was tempted to run over, to tell them everything. But then it occurred to him that he might have committed a crime at Fabricon. He'd as good as broken into the place, and he'd stolen some clothing and set off an alarm. The police would-n't believe his story. Fabricon had a good reputation. And who was he?

All the same, he was sure there was something wrong at the computer firm. His friends *had* looked like zombies. If he hadn't seen them being brainwashed, what *had* he seen? Maybe his grandfather would have the answer.

Now he turned and saw the man coming on. A tall man, dark-haired, lithe, and almost handsome. He did-n't look like a killer. But then he was from Fabricon.

The man was about half a block away. Tom thought, *The guy won't grab me in front of a police car.*

At the same time he was aware that a lot could happen under the noses of the police.

The light changed and he jogged across the street. A burly cop eyed him as he passed but seemed to have little interest. At least there was no alarm out. *Of course there isn't! Fabricon can't risk it!*

Tom struggled to catch his breath. Hollis Street loomed ahead, the downtown section, a tangle of light and shadow, a pandemonium of cars and trucks. A bus roared by, impatient drivers leaned on their horns, and pedestrians hurried home, loaded down with parcels.

All these ordinary people, Tom realized, knew nothing; they had no idea of what was happening. They would be the first to want him thrown in jail for his escapade. "We need Fabricon," they would say. "We don't need crazy kids stirring things up!"

Tom came out on Hollis, took a quick look over his shoulder, and saw the man coming on.

But now he had an idea of how to shake him. He dashed across at the light, jogged past a candy store and a photo shop, then ducked through the doors of Zinser's Five and Dime.

It was a busy place, but shabby at the edges, open late to snare more customers. The smell of lunch counter grease, of popcorn, seemed to hang in the air, settling on the cheap dresses, the imitation leather, and the fake jewellery.

Tom made his way quickly between the aisles. In here, he didn't feel conspicuous. Nobody looked very prosperous, and nobody seemed to notice him — which was exactly what he was counting on.

Tom had worked at Zinser's for one miserable weekend, before he called his grandfather and begged him to let him quit. The store manager had been a nasty brute who made him lift huge boxes, cut his lunch hour, and sneered at his acne.

As a result of his brief stint, though, Tom knew that Zinser's back entrance ran into a parking lot on Madison Street, the next one over from Hollis. The Madison Street bus ran south and passed within two blocks of his grandfather's.

Tom took a deep breath, pushed through the double doors at the end of the main aisle, and walked boldly into the gloomy inner sanctum. A fat man behind a desk growled at him.

"What can I do for you, kid?"

"Uh … sorry. My little brother, I think he ran out this way."

Not stopping to gauge the man's reaction, Tom dashed between piled boxes and racks of clothing, dodged a couple of trash cans, and reached the back entrance.

As he stumbled into the crowded parking lot, he thought, *Now the guy in black will track me. He'll find out I've gone this way and get right after me. If only I can catch a bus. … Who is this guy?* The question pounded in his brain, took on the rhythm of his motion. He must have been watching Fabricon the whole time. He was waiting there, outside, confident that Tom would reappear.

Why hadn't he just come in to nail him there?

He ran two blocks along Madison. There was no way he could stand and wait, even though there was no sign of his pursuer. Minutes later, a bus came lurching along and Tom climbed gratefully in. The vehicle was full of shoppers, a few older people, and mothers with their children.

It was the first time he had felt safe in quite a while.

He got off the bus and walked the two blocks to his grandfather's. It wasn't that late yet, and he was sure he'd find the old man up. He hoped he was in a good mood and that he hadn't had too much grog after dinner.

Tom rang the doorbell, waited, and then rang again. The house lights were on and he thought he heard the sound of harmonica music.

He pounded on the door and heard groanings and mumblings inside — his grandfather's voice.

Suddenly the door was flung open and Jack Sandalls, red-eyed and blustering, stood gaping at him.

"Tom! What in hell are you doing here?"

Tom shrank back. He felt awkward and foolish. But, almost immediately, Jack's gaze softened.

"Well, come on in, son. Don't let all the hot air of the city get in my place."

Jack shut the door, flashing a slightly uneasy smile as he held up his famous harmonica.

"Musical evening," he explained.

Tom, who could smell the alcohol on his breath, smiled and nodded.

His grandfather claimed he could play everything from "Stars and Stripes Forever" to "Liebestraum" on the harmonica, although Tom had only ever heard "Blow the Man Down," and that only when his grandfather had had a few, which was clearly the case this evening.

As they walked toward the kitchen, Jack leaned over and whispered into Tom's ear. "Got a little company tonight. Maid's night off, you know."

He winked. Tom winced but tried to get into the spirit of things. "I'm glad you're having fun, Grandpa."

At the same time he was thinking, *I need help badly and Grandpa's gone and got drunk. I shouldn't have come here. What am I going to do now?*

"I'd like to call my mom," he said.

"You can call her in a minute, Tommy boy. Come and say good night to Maisie first."

Maisie, one of the two owners of the house, was a large woman with flowing white hair, lively eyes, and a striking hooked nose. She seemed to take up a lot of space and had a Mother Hubbard air about her that made Tom a little uneasy. When he first met her he had commented to his grandfather about the nose.

"Gives her character," Jack had assured him

As Tom came into the kitchen, Maisie stood up. Wobbling a little, she greeted him with a warm, slightly glassy-eyed smile.

The remains of a meal lay on the kitchen table — a roast, bits of bread, an enormous pie, a couple of half-empty wine bottles, and several crumpled paper napkins.

"Maisie brought me over a wonderful dinner. Help yourself to some pie," Jack said.

Tom found suddenly that he was starving. He gobbled down some pie.

"I'm on my way," Maisie said and took a couple of uneasy steps across the kitchen.

Jack took her arm. "I'll just see my guest home, Tom. You make your phone call. Stay the night if you want. You look like you could use a good sleep."

"A wash, too, if it comes to that," Maisie said. "Not that he isn't a handsome one under all that dirt."

"Takes after his grandfather," Jack said, winking at him. The old man and Maisie disappeared, amid much giggling and guffawing, in the direction of the front door. Tom sprang upon the phone and dialled his mother's number.

It rang a few times, and then he heard a man's voice on the other end. Reichert.

He wanted to hang up. Instead, he held the phone at arm's length for a minute and swore.

Reichert said, "Hello? Hello?"

"Can I speak to my mother?"

"Oh, it's you, guy? Your mother was wondering where you were. You didn't call earlier, did you?"

"No. Why?"

"Oh, we've just been getting a few phone calls this evening — with nobody on the other end. Some nut, I guess. Here's your mother."

Tom felt helpless, angry. At the same time he was afraid. Who'd been phoning the apartment? But when his mother came on, an unexpected rage overwhelmed him.

"Why is he there again? Do you have to see Reichert all the time?"

"Tom, don't be upset. You and I have to have a nice long talk."

"You always say that, but we never do. Besides, I don't want to talk."

"You mustn't be hard on me, Tom. This heat wave's got us all exhausted. You know what Chuck's gone and done? He's found us two nice fans — they've already done wonders to cool everything down here."

The words got out before Tom could stop them. "Is that so he can hang around there even more?"

"Tom, I'm disappointed."

There was a long pause. Tom wiped his forehead and swallowed hard.

"Sorry, Mom."

"Hey, that's much better. Now I've got to tell you before I forget. Willy called from Damato's and he wants you to come in tomorrow. You're feeling OK, aren't you? I got your note. Did you go to a movie?"

"I decided not to." He hesitated, and then, suddenly inspired, told her, "I just went over to check out Fabricon."

"Oh, I'm glad. I've heard it's a great place to work. Jemmie was saying that her nephew just got hired there. It sounds like a great opportunity, Tom. Did you talk to anyone?"

"A few people. There's nothing definite. Listen, Mom, I'd like to stay at Grandpa's tonight."

"OK."

The OK came a little too quickly for Tom's liking. "Listen, Mom, make sure the door is locked tonight," he said.

"You mean the phone calls? Don't worry about them. Just some crank. If you decide to come over later, wake me up. We can have a late-night chat, if you like."

"That sounds great, but I think I'll stay here, Mom. I'll come over and get my clothes in the morning."

Tom hung up feeling much closer to his mother. She always seemed to soothe his worst fears. But what were his worst fears in this case? Reichert was disgusting, but tonight he had other worries. He had a terrible feeling that there would be some bad repercussions over his visit to Fabricon.

He had a crazy idea that it was the man in black who was making the phone calls. But how could that be, since the man couldn't possibly know who he was?

Jack returned and started clearing up the kitchen. He was good at pulling himself together, even after a lot of drinks. He put on a kettle to boil and lit his pipe, then looked at Tom questioningly and waited.

"Something's up, Grandpa," Tom said, collapsing into a chair by the wood stove.

"Oh, I can see that all right. Don't tell me you've gone and robbed a store."

"Sorry I arrived out of the blue, but I've got to talk to you."

"So talk."

Tom hesitated and got started slowly. He talked about his impressions of his friends, about Fabricon, about the night's adventure and the man in black. He didn't mention sending away for the Mercury Man ring. That seemed to have taken place in another world, a world of crazy dreams and speculations. All of a sudden he had run head-on into reality. He had entered a space where there were no superheroes and no magic rings — just powerful forces whose secrets you mustn't even think about.

When he had finished, his grandfather stopped to relight his pipe. He asked a few questions, listened patiently to Tom's answers, then cleared his throat and said, "The problem is I'm not sure I believe all of it. And if I don't believe it, who else will?"

Tom jumped up to protest. "But, Grandpa!"

"Just a minute! I'm not saying you're lying to me, son. I know you wouldn't do that. What I'm trying to get across to you is that there's a lot of speculation here. You don't really know that your friends were being hypnotized or brainwashed, do you?"

"But I saw them!"

"You caught a glimpse from a balcony. That's not enough! There's no proof of anything. And think about it. Why should an up-and-coming computer company brainwash a bunch of kids? Even assuming they could do it, it doesn't make sense. Why risk their reputation for such a small return? To get a few kids hyped up on the company? It's just crazy!"

"But Grandpa, you must have heard about Dr. Tarn. He's been in the newspapers — one of MIT's geniuses, they say. He has a lot of weird theories on the brain. He might be doing some kind of mind experiment, or even using kids in his research because he thinks what he's doing is important enough to justify anything."

Jack shook his head. "The evil genius idea, huh? And what about Binkley, the CEO? You think he'd just go along? C'mon, Tom, there's got to be a better explanation than that."

"All I know is what I saw."

"You could have been mistaken in what you saw. I'll tell you, Tom — the thing that might make it stick is the man in black. I think he's the key to the whole thing. The only trouble is that his actions don't make sense."

"What do you mean?"

"Why would he be waiting around outside? Once he got you in the building he'd be in there to make sure you stuck. Are you sure this guy was following you?"

"Grandpa!"

"All right, all right, you're sure. Then I guess you might see him again, and if you do, you're going to have to go right up and talk to him."

"What?"

"I don't mean in a dark alley, of course. But in a public street, why not? You have a right to ask him why he's trailing you. I just wish I could be there when you confront him."

"You think he'll show up again?"

"If he's part of some conspiracy, sure. You might not be too difficult to trace."

Tom shivered. "Grandpa, someone was phoning the apartment tonight. Mom told me. But they hung up without speaking."

Jack's look was grave. "I would expect something like that. If he gets through when you're there alone, talk to him. Then let me know right away. Now look, we both have to think things out. You need some rest and so do I. You go and clean up, have a shower, and I'll set up the sofa in the office for you. We'll talk more about this over breakfast."

As soon as his grandfather suggested this, Tom realized how exhausted he was. Even so, he dragged himself to the shower, while Jack sat smoking and drinking coffee, looking grave and preoccupied.

When Tom finished in the bathroom he found the bed in the office laid out with clean sheets and a pillow. His grandfather stood at the door and said quietly, "Try to get some rest. Nobody's going to bother you here. I'll try to sleep on this. We'll work out a strategy over breakfast."

But Tom sat up, restless, hearing sounds all around the house and out in yard. A couple of times he went to the window and peered into the semi-darkness, expecting a figure to rise from the skeletal lilac bush. Finally, he took down his grandfather's Mercury Man comics and began to read them through. When he got to the fourth comic, the one in which Mercury Man was about to foil the Nazis at a California airplane factory, he fell asleep.

Chapter Six

The Pursuit Continues

"Two hash coming up!" shouted Fast-Fry Willy from the window. A couple of customers looked up hopefully. Willy's hash and scrapple were famous. Tom wiped the counter and stared out beyond the neon and the slatted blinds at the grey street. Nothing suspicious was happening out there — it was just another grubby morning on the east side, enlivened as usual by the smell of good food and strong coffee, the rumble of conversation and laughter, the flare of cigarettes being lit like candles in the smoky den that was Damato's.

And across the room and through the smoke Tom saw a reassuring sight: his grandfather at a corner table, reading a tabloid and slyly watching the door for any sign of a stranger.

Tom worked up front at Damato's Diner, but not regularly, because the two behind-the-counter men, Fast-Fry Willy and Singapore, were almost never absent. When he really needed the money Tom would sometimes fill in for one of the kitchen guys, but mostly he liked it at the front.

The diner was actually an old place from the forties, looking a bit like a shabby boxcar but fixed up enough to pass the health and fire regulations, if only just. It had air conditioning, after a fashion, and an unflappable waitress named Hester, who never let a coffee cup get less than three-quarters full.

Nobody seemed to know who owned the restaurant — it certainly wasn't anybody named Damato — and nobody much cared. It was located on the edge of Mechanicstown, near the Greyhound bus station, and populated by old men who complained about enlarging prostates and shrinking horizons, a few tight-lipped Vietnam vets, various winos and ex-acidheads, non-fastidious cleaning ladies, slick men who ran pawnshops, busted policemen, and small-time delivery drivers.

Tom was good with most of these people because he knew how to listen. Only rarely did any of the patrons ask him embarrassing questions, such as: "Are you gonna spend your whole life pouring coffee?" "What's your dad do, anyway?" "What's the name of your girlfriend?"

That morning he had woken early and he and his grandfather had gone together to the apartment so he could change his clothes and check things out. His mother, already at work, had left a note that said, "Maybe we could have a pizza together tonight? Love you."

There had been nothing suspicious around the building. No sign of Fabricon. No man in black watching. Tom was beginning to feel more easy. Yesterday was receding a bit, like a bad dream.

Around nine-thirty the diner crowd thinned out. A few of the old codgers hung around and talked to his grandfather. Hester the waitress had settled down at her time-out table to do a crossword and have a smoke. One or two messengers came in for takeouts.

Then a police car stopped by, and Tom, suddenly fearful, ducked into the back — but the cop, a bulky, red-faced man whom he knew as a regular, only wanted donuts.

It was all right then, it seemed. Nothing was going to happen. Relaxed, Tom was drinking a juice and trying to read the sports pages when he looked up and saw Estella and Pete coming through the diner door.

This was crazy! The kids never came over here!

Tom watched them, mustering a wan smile, wondering what in hell they wanted with him.

"Hey, Tom! How's the hangover?" Pete Halloran greeted him loudly and jokingly as he plumped down on a counter stool right beside the cash. He waved to Estella, who had seemed to hang back, and she too sat down, giving Tom a gentle once-over.

They ordered coffee, and Pete began the conversation on a noncommittal note.

"So how's it going?"

Tom shrugged his shoulders. He was trying not to stare. These were his friends — but were they? Hadn't he seen them hustling into Fabricon to be given Dr. Tarn's brainwashing treatment? Could he trust them now?

"OK," he said. "Everything's just fine."

A couple of years ago, he remembered, he and Pete used to sit in coffee shops and talk about UFOs, portholes, extraterrestrial life, and the fate of the galaxy. In those days Pete was fat and eager and a bit naive, but he had changed. He'd been working out and had developed some muscle. Now he was dressing in cool clothes, had his driver's licence, and was dropping in on the local gambling places with his girlfriends.

There was a kind of bluster about Pete these days that seemed to go down well with most people, but Tom didn't like it. Still, they played pool sometimes, and Tom had decided he really wasn't such a bad guy at heart.

"How come you showed up here? You guys never come here."

Tom looked from one to the other, then at his grandfather, who was watching from the corner. Was that slight nod of his head a signal of encouragement? Tom had promised to keep his cool no matter what happened and to take his cue from Jack.

"We wanted to see you," Estella said. "To have a talk with you."

That sounded innocuous enough, but then Pete said, with a kind of smirk, "You been doing a little exploring, Tom?"

Tom looked at him. "What do you mean by that?"

"We were getting a briefing at Fabricon last night," Estella told him. "We heard that some kid broke into the place. He was recorded on the security cameras. Dr. Tarn asked Pete and me to come in and look at the tapes and we had to identify you."

"Thanks a lot!"

Tom felt sick. They knew who he was and they were going to go after him!

"It isn't our fault," Estella protested. "We had to tell him! Somebody else would have recognized you. Besides, they're going to be nice about it. They're not going to prosecute."

"Dr. Tarn's a cool guy. He's not going to go after you, Tom. He just wants to talk to you."

"Why didn't you come with us, Tom? I don't understand it!" Estella said. "They would have hired you like a shot. You're good with computers."

"I don't want to talk to Tarn at all," Tom protested. He was frightened. If he let Fabricon come near him, there was no telling what they'd do!

His grandfather had picked up on his agitation. The old man watched closely and stirred in his seat, but he didn't get up.

"Dr. Tarn's doing you a real favour," Pete insisted. "What in heck were you doing over there anyway?"

The door of the diner opened and a man came in. A tall man in a white T-shirt, shorts, and dark sunglasses. Tom could see his fancy silver racing bike where he'd locked it up by the fire hydrant. Hester took his order and Tom had to get some juice and coffee. Fast-Fry Willy, who was having a smoke in the back, got up to do an order of eggs and scrapple.

"I just wanted to check the place out," Tom said. "You guys were talking like it was paradise or something. Then somebody started to chase me and I panicked. I'll pay for any damage, but I don't want to go to Fabricon."

Pete's broad smirk turned into laughter.

"Tarn said you were in a disguise, that you broke into a private room. You been reading the Hardy Boys or something?"

Tom gritted his teeth. "Let me ask you this: what were you guys doing at Fabricon last night?"

"We all went over in a company van," Estella said. "They treated us great. We got a tour of some of the advanced labs and met some of the marketing people."

"Fabricon's all over the world," Pete said. "They've got incredible plans for the future, too."

"Yeah? You saw a film, didn't you. They showed you some kind of film."

"That was the boring part," Estella said.

"The film was nothing," Pete insisted. "It was just some stuff they were testing. Soothing sounds and weird pictures, like some of those modern paintings. They wanted to try it out on us. I can't even remember it, really."

"Why are you asking us this?" Estella cradled her coffee cup, staring at Tom intently with her dark eyes. Then she turned suddenly and noticed Jack Sandalls, who was by this time shifting uneasily in the corner. She waved and the old man nodded. "How come you're getting so standoffish, Tom?" Estella continued. "And so suspicious? You used to be upfront about everything."

"I just don't like the feel of Fabricon," he said. Then he remembered the mysterious phone calls to his home. "Did you guys try to call me last night?"

"No," said Estella. "Of course not. Tarn asked us not to." This was not the answer Tom had hoped for. He was still uneasy about the calls.

His concern was interrupted when he suddenly became aware of the tall man in the sunglasses standing beside him.

"If you're not reading that paper, kid, I wouldn't mind a look." The man's voice was deep and almost sullen.

Tom handed him the newspaper. As the man retreated, he stared absent-mindedly after him. All of a sudden he caught his breath.

Had he seen that walk and manner before? He couldn't be sure. Not here, anyway. Last night?

He cast a desperate look in the direction of his grandfather, but Jack was talking to one of his cronies, not looking in Tom's direction.

Why didn't Grandfather see him? Why didn't he react? I must be imagining things. Why should the man in black come here? Tarn's sent word already, through the kids. Besides, it doesn't look like him. The man last night was slimmer. But maybe it was the running suit. God! I can't remember exactly …

"What's the matter with you, Tom, are you going weird?" Pete asked him. "All of sudden you look sick. Must be the smoke in this place. Jeez! You've got to get it together or you're going to lose out on all your chances. Stuff is happening around this city and you're just missing the boat."

"Give Doc Tarn a call," Estella told him. "He told us to pass along his card to you. Said everything would be cool, so long as he hears from you right away."

"You know Tarn personally?"

Pete laughed. "Sure we do, Tom. Hell, he's a good guy. Looks like you nearly struck out with the company, though."

Fast-Fry Willy, a slender, wrinkled apparition, coffee-coloured and wearing a white apron, deposited a plate of scrapple, bacon, and eggs on the counter.

"One eggs and scrapple, Hester. Can I get you kids something?" he asked.

Pete made a wry face. "No thanks."

Willy disappeared, and as Hester waddled across to get the plate, Pete leaned over and whispered to Tom. "Man, what's that stuff with the eggs and bacon? I just hope you don't eat it yourself. You should try the cafeteria at Fabricon. Best fast food in the city."

"Screw you. Willy's a great cook. His scrapple is terrific."

Pete shrugged his shoulders.

"I think it's time to take off, Estella. Give Tommy the card and let's get back to Fabricon. He likes to hang out with the rummies and the downbeats."

Tom was trying to get his grandfather's attention. He took the calling card from Estella without even looking at it. The tall man had his back to him, busy over his breakfast. *I must be mistaken. It couldn't be the same man.*

"Why don't you come over to Fabricon with us?" Estella asked. "We'll stick by you and make it OK with Dr. Tarn."

"We'll even hold your hand," Pete added. "Of course if they decide to prosecute, we'll forget we ever knew you."

He laughed and Estella turned and shoved at him.

"Lay off, will you? ... What about it, can you get away right now, Tom?"

"I can't." Tom had managed to signal his grandfather. Jack was coming slowly toward him, his coffee cup held out carefully like a chalice. "I've got the card. I'll think about calling him, don't worry."

"We're off, then," Pete announced. He started to retreat in the direction of the door. Estella followed slowly, waving to Pete's grandfather as she took off.

"Bye, Mr. Sandalls."

Jack waved to her. He came straight up to the counter, set his coffee cup down, and said in a loud voice, "So we're gonna put a little bet on the baseball game, are we, kid?"

Tom gaped at him, and the old man said under his breath, "That guy sitting over there with the breakfast ... I'm wondering if he's the man who was following you last night. Did you have a feeling about him, maybe?"

"Maybe ... but I just don't know!"

Jack winked, turned around, and took a turn around the room. In one corner three women were having coffee. Nearby, a messenger was chewing on a sandwich. Jack's cronies sat in another corner. They had begun a game of cards and were joking about some woman they knew. The tall man sat at a table near the door. He seemed to be devoting all his attention to his breakfast, which he had already almost disposed of.

Jack strolled past him, stopped, and turned back casually to the table.

"Excuse me," he said, "you wouldn't be old Jess Hiram's nephew, now, would you? The one that went off to study engineering in Chicago?"

The man raised his head very slowly. He gave Jack a moment's searching look, then turned back to his food. His look and manner reminded Tom of one of those silent strangers in a western.

"Never heard of him," the man said in his deep monotone voice. Then he simply ignored Jack — it was as if he had made him disappear.

The old sea captain, however, was not going to be put off so easily.

"Oh, I just wondered. Haven't seen you in here before, you know. Most of us are regulars, like. Guess you know a good place when you see it."

"The *breakfast* is very good," the man said. "But as a matter of fact, I'm on my way."

He stood up so suddenly that Jack saw his grandfather startle back.

The man smiled and picked up the newspaper. He drank the remains of his coffee. Hester lumbered over with his check and he brought it straight to the counter, where Tom stood watching him with pounding heart.

A man, slender and muscular, thirty-five years old, maybe forty. With dark eyebrows and dark eyes, thin lips, high cheekbones, and a strong Roman nose.

The man counted out the $3.50 for the breakfast, picked up a toothpick from the holder, and turned away.

Then he stopped, turned back, and laid the folded newspaper on the counter.

"Thanks, kid," he said, and walked back to get his sunglasses, then straight out the door, not looking at Jack at all, although the latter managed a faint "So long" as the stranger passed him.

Tom's grandfather, shaking his head, wandered back to the counter.

"I don't think that was him, Grandpa," Tom said. "There was something about this guy that was different. Anyway — I've got to tell you! Dr. Tarn wants to see me. They spotted me on the video cameras. You've got to help me! I just don't know what to do."

Jack started to speak, unconsciously folding back the newspaper as he did so. He and Tom looked down at the same time and saw the small torn sheet fluttering out of it. The man, who had already climbed on his bicycle and disappeared, must have slipped it in there.

Tom snatched at the paper and saw that there was writing on it, one sentence, printed neatly in pencil. He held it up and read it to his grandfather.

Why are you watching Fabricon? it said.

CHAPTER SEVEN

The Gospel According to Tarn

Jack Sandalls gave a low whistle, walked over, and opened the diner door. He peered up and down the street, as if he were trying to conjure the man back by some magic.

"So that's what he looked like," he said, returning slowly to the counter. He patted Tom reassuringly on the shoulder. "Well, at least we've got his number now. He won't surprise us again."

Tom shook his head. He felt miserable. He knew a threat hung over him and he could only look nervously from side to side and wonder what Fabricon would do next. His grandfather's calm was not reassuring; it almost made things worse. The old man seemed to be out of it. Neither of them would be a match for the company once they started moving in.

And it seemed they had already started.

Tom had a sudden fantasy of running away. He had a cousin he barely knew in northern Minnesota.

That might be far enough away. Maybe it was time to think of leaving West Hope. But his mother — what would she think about all this? He had a vision of her marching over to Fabricon and telling them bluntly to leave her son alone. But of course she would blame him for sneaking in there; she would tell him just to forget his suspicions. They couldn't really be doing anything to his friends. It was just his imagination, like all that stuff about portholes, other realities, space beings.

"We have to work out a plan," Jack said. He had seated himself at the counter, facing Tom, and helped himself to another cup of coffee. He looked very wrinkled and old, red-eyed, and much too unshaven, and his white hair was a tousled mess. Tom found his cool manner almost maddening.

"It's hard to know what to do," Jack said. "First the company sends the card through Pete and Estella, and now this guy comes snooping around. It's clear that they have something to hide. I have to hand it to you, Tom, you seem to be on to something."

"You didn't believe me before, Grandpa?"

"Oh, it's not that I didn't believe what you told me. It's just that I thought your interpretation might be wrong. Now I wonder. They seem mighty anxious to get to you. I can't figure out why they sent this guy over here, though. They haven't even given you time to answer their invitation."

"I don't want to see Tarn, Grandpa. I don't want to go to Fabricon."

"I can understand that, but you can't just put your head in the sand. I was thinking — what about you call Tarn's office and invite him over here? You and I can see him together and find out what's on his plate. Maybe everything has a simple explanation. Maybe he's somehow doing all your friends a favour. Maybe you'll want to hook up with him yourself."

"Never! I hated that place!" Tom's voice was suddenly too loud. Hester the waitress and a few patrons looked over.

"Easy does it," Jack said. "You can do what you want, but with somebody like that jogger fellow on your track, I suggest you get right on that phone and talk to Tarn's office. If he's really got something on his mind he'll come here, and then maybe we can get everything settled. You can't go around with this guy shadowing you all the time."

"God, what am I going to tell Mom?"

"The truth — or else nothing. You might want to wait until we've seen Tarn. That might save her quite a bit of worry. See if he can come over this afternoon."

Tom set the card on the counter and stared at it as if it might give him the courage to take some action. The shiny cardboard with its raised lettering looked so clean and neat and professional. It made him feel unimportant and powerless. He hated calling official places — schools and stores and offices. And now he had to call the famous Dr. Tarn. And there was no telling what would happen when he did.

He moved along the counter to where the phone was. All the customers were oblivious of his fears, drinking coffee, smoking, and chattering together, jogging steadily through life. He could hear Willy singing away to himself in the kitchen. For him, too, everything was smooth and normal. And for Hester, and his mother, and even his poor brainwashed friends, who couldn't remember what they'd seen in that Fabricon film.

Was it such a big deal to dial a number? It was. His grandfather was watching him. He dialled.

A couple of rings, then a smooth-voiced secretary said, "Fabricon Computers. Dr. Tarn's office. How can I help you?"

Tom told her who he was, and she went on in the same smooth manner. "Oh, yes, Dr. Tarn wanted to see you. May I make an appointment for later today? What time? Right. Where? Damato's Cafe? I'll have to check on that. Is there a number there I could call?"

Ten minutes later the counter phone rang and the smooth voice confirmed that Dr. Tarn would be dropping by Damato's at two-thirty. He looked forward to meeting Mr. Tom Blake and Mr. Sandalls.

When Tom explained this, his grandfather rubbed his hands together.

"Now we have to plan some strategy," he said.

He disappeared into the back of the diner and came back with a pen and some sheets of paper.

"Let's sit down and work things out," he said. "Willy is going to take over the counter for you, just so long as you can help with the lunch crowd."

They found a table by the door, and Jack began to make a kind of log sheet. Carefully, he set down "known facts," and beside this "possibilities," and in another column "actions and possible results."

Tom was amazed at the old man's thoroughness. He usually thought of his grandfather as pretty eccentric, forgetting that he had been a sea captain and sailed good-sized ships in and out of some of the world's biggest seaports.

After they had everything down on paper and had gone over it a few times, Tom felt much better. By that time the diner was filling up with the lunch crowd — couriers and drivers, river guys, local storekeepers, and the usual array of hairdressers, off-duty waitresses, and a few cool women shopping for bargains in the charity stores.

Tom was kept busy; he had almost no time to think. Then, suddenly, the crowd was gone, the hands of the clock had turned 'round, and it was nearly time for the arrival of Dr. Tarn. Tom took a last look at the notes his grandfather had made and kept his glance expectantly on the street outside.

The counter phone rang suddenly and he grabbed it.

"Is that you, Tom?"

It was Estella. Tom quickly explained that they would be seeing Tarn in a few minutes.

"That's great. You see, I told you he was an OK guy. Since when do big executives and scientists show up in diners to talk to teenagers?"

"It might mean he has something to be afraid of."

"Hey, Tom. Everything's going to be cool now, right? You know there's a little thing tonight at Bim's. Why don't you come over? You could give us the scoop on Tarn and we could fill you in on Fabricon. How about it?"

Tom winced. He was glad to be invited but he knew he wouldn't go. He liked hanging around with his friends for things like movies and conversation — but the whole girl-boy party scene made him scared and uncomfortable. On that circuit nobody seemed natural: everything was crazy, loud, and competitive, and even the girls he liked were hard to take. And since he didn't smoke dope there was nothing to smooth things out. This was how he felt, although his feelings embarrassed him. He felt left out and bit like a failure.

"Thanks for the invitation," he said. "Maybe I'll come — but right now I have to concentrate on Tarn."

"OK. Sure ..." She sounded a little disappointed. "Hey, Tom. You know that film showing you mentioned? I almost forgot, but there *was* something kind of funny about it."

"What do you mean?"

"Well, they did a kind of test before the whole thing. They showed us some swirls and patterns and played some music, and some kids were chosen to watch the film while others were taken off to do something else. I don't know why they did that."

"Neither do I. Thanks for telling me that."

"See you tonight, Tom."

"Yeah ... maybe. Thanks."

As he put down the phone he remembered that his mother wanted to give him dinner that evening. He had no idea what he would say to her. Of course Reichert might show up and spoil things — he seemed to be doing that a lot recently.

Tom took off his apron, glanced at himself in the mirror, pushed his hair back. His grandfather, ensconced at a corner table, waved to him.

A blue Mercedes convertible had just pulled up at the diner door.

Tom recognized Dr. Tarn immediately. Despite the heat he was wearing a dark blue suit, sunglasses, and a panama hat, and he carried the same small black briefcase that Tom had seen the previous night.

Shutting the car door, Tarn paused to look up and down the street, after which his glance roved over Damato's, seeming to take in the whole place, right down to the missing letter in the old neon window sign. Tom wondered if anyone had ever cast such a sharp look at the diner.

Tom waved at his grandfather, walked around the counter, and met the scientist as he pushed through the heavy door.

"Ah, you must be the young Mr. Blake," the man said, holding out his hand. He was not very tall, but he seemed strongly built, with broad shoulders and restless, massive hands. When he took off his sunglasses Tom saw that he had penetrating dark blue eyes.

"Willis Tarn of Fabricon. I'm glad to meet you."

Tom shook hands with the scientist and Tarn greeted Jack, who had come over to join them.

"Let's sit down over here," Jack said. "Can I get you some coffee, Dr. Tarn?"

"No thank you, but a glass of juice would be nice."

Tarn sat down, took off his hat, and set it on the table. He wiped his forehead decorously with the palm of his hand. His balding head, Tom noticed, was bullet-shaped and large, while his cheeks seemed to bloom with rosy health.

"Interesting place," the scientist said, looking around at Damato's.

Jack brought over an orange juice and Tarn proceeded to ask them both a few polite questions. Did they live together? How was Tom getting on in school? Did he want to go to university? How was his mother doing?

The questions were nothing unusual, but Tom felt restless and uneasy. He longed for the scientist to get to the point. Then, without any transition, between one sip of juice and the next, he did.

"Now what on earth caused a fine young fellow like you to break into Fabricon?" Tarn asked. The question was gently put, but the man's eyes were unsmiling.

Tom and his grandfather had rehearsed this one carefully. They had decided not to mention the stranger in the jogging suit. "Never let the other side know what you know," his grandfather had said. They hoped that Tarn would let something slip that would reveal whether or not the dark stranger was really a company hireling.

"I was walking down Harbour Street to the amusement park," Tom said, "and I saw a bunch of my friends come up in a van in front of Fabricon. I was kind of shy to go right up to them, but when they disappeared inside I decided to go in and have a look."

"Aaah. … And you were too shy to announce your-self at the front desk, I suppose. Just wandered into the place, is that it?"

"That's it. When I got in there I got scared and thought somebody might arrest me for trespassing. So I put on a cleaner's outfit and tried to sneak out, but I went into the wrong place."

"You went into Copernicus Hall. A funny place to choose. And what did you see there?"

Tom swallowed hard. "There was some kind of movie. I guess it was one of your training promos. I've heard a lot about your training program."

"Only you don't want to be part of it! Why is that, Thomas?"

Tom shook his head. "I don't know. I really don't know."

"You haven't heard bad things about Fabricon?"

"No, sir. Not at all."

"Nobody's come to you and complained about Fabricon? None of your friends? No stranger?"

"No, sir."

"You just decided to take a look and got in over your head, is that it?"

"Yes, sir."

"Tell me, Thomas, when you caught a glimpse of the training film — did it arouse your interest in Fabricon? Did you like what you saw?"

"I didn't actually see much of the film," Tom told him. He felt that there was a trap in this question some-where, but he couldn't exactly figure where.

He looked at his grandfather and detected a slight nod of encouragement — he wasn't sure if Tarn had seen it also.

"It was dark and I got scared," he went on. "A couple of guys came after me. I just caught a glimpse of these funny patterns. It was like some kind of modern cartoon thing."

"Did you listen to the narrative?"

"I — I can't remember. There was a lot of stuff about Fabricon, about the future of the company — then the guys came and grabbed me."

"Did you catch a glimpse of your friends at all? Were they enjoying the presentation?"

"I didn't see them — I just saw the screen. It was dark and I was scared."

Dr. Tarn peered at him. "Interesting. It was reported to me that you were there long enough to get a good look at the film and the audience."

Jack shifted in his seat, cleared his throat, and looked pointedly at Tarn.

The scientist didn't return his glance, but his tone suddenly changed.

"You have to understand, young man, that Fabricon operates in a very competitive industry. We pay huge sums to hire people with ideas and we expect them to be loyal. Corporate espionage isn't unknown in the industry, and we're quite upset when we feel that one of our special programs might be compromised."

Jack laughed harshly and shifted in his chair. "You don't think our Tom's been paid by somebody to spy on you, do you, Dr. Tarn? Why, he wouldn't know the first thing about ripping off your secrets! And if you're inviting all the teenage kids in the city in, why should you care about one more?" He raised his eyes to the ceiling, as if protesting this absurdity.

Tarn shrugged his shoulders. "We have to keep alert to all the possibilities, Captain Sandalls. We like to control our own environment. We can't just have people — not even innocent teenagers — dropping in when they feel like it."

"I didn't mean to cause any trouble," Tom said. He was glad to hear Tarn say "innocent."

"I'm sure you didn't." The scientist paused, glanced briefly at his watch, and continued. "Perhaps you'd understand better if I told you something of the vision we have at Fabricon. We're much more than a profit-making organization. Although we are that, we are that."

Tarn's look grew intense. It seemed to sweep past Tom and his grandfather, to soar beyond the narrow streets, the grim buildings, the sweating city.

"You see, my two friends, the old world we all know is fading away. In that world, human communication was limited to the personal, the trivial, the idiosyncratic. Soon that kind of communication will be as dead as the dinosaurs. All over this planet, more and more people are becoming part of the great world information link."

As he spoke, Tarn's right hand slid across the table. He extracted a sugar cube from the cracked bowl and methodically began to unwrap it. He seemed to be doing this unconsciously, but Tom found the gesture distracting, even a little disturbing.

"The brain, as is now clear, was nothing but nature's first effort at making a computer, a communications instrument that would girdle the planet. A crude effort, repeated in each human body, but just successful enough so that this meat machine we carry around on our shoulders was able to find a way to go beyond its limitations."

Tom saw his grandfather wince a little at the term "meat machine."

"All the minds of the world are becoming one mind. We're witnessing the beginning of what I call the Great Conversation — people from all over the planet linked up and becoming interested in the same things. Look at how television has brought the whole world together. Now computer companies like Fabricon are shaping the new agenda for the human race."

As he spoke, Tarn's forehead, wrinkled and shining, seemed to expand in the glaring light. The sugar cube moved between his fingers as if he were a conjurer.

"Cybernetics is working on one front to supersede the crude human brain. On another front, it's becoming clear that human beings are just animals completely programmed by their genetic inheritance. We have no real freedom of choice, and in the long run we can't expect to survive unless we let ourselves be guided by the information machines we've created. We have to escape from all the old half-baked ideas about soul and personality and spirit. To make ourselves the servants of the greatest force for good this planet has ever known — the ultra-intelligent computer. And every step we take at linking people to a communications network takes us closer to realizing that."

Jack shifted uneasily in his chair. "You mean you believe people count for nothing? You want us to give up thinking for ourselves and just learn everything from the machines we've created?"

"Of course I don't want us to give up thinking, Captain Sandalls. The trouble is that human thinking is too limited. And so is human biology. We need to be rescued from our genetic misprintings, our deviations and irrationalities — not to mention our diseases and psychoses. Then we'll begin to have dominion over this planet, as the Bible says we should. In fact, it's our only hope for survival."

As Tarn said this he crushed the small sugar cube between his fingers.

Jack gave a low whistle. "Well, what you say may be what we need, Dr. Tarn, but I sure hope I'm not around to see it happen."

Tarn looked at him and laughed. "I can't expect an old freebooter like you to enjoy these prospects. But the young people understand where we're going. It doesn't really matter what us old fogies think."

Tarn cast Tom a benevolent look. "You've been talking to your friends, haven't you? Surely they've conveyed the excitement in their own way? Or perhaps you got a glimpse of this on your brief visit?"

Tom sensed that they were getting to the crunch.

Tarn leaned forward, his blue eyes narrowed. "Why not come over and join us for an evening? I know your friends have already invited you. I think Fabricon would be quite willing to forget your little intrusion if you'd give us a chance to show you what we really are."

Tom hadn't expected this. There was no way he would go back inside that building! He turned to his grandfather with a desperate look.

But the old man seemed unalarmed.

"What do you say, Tom? Dr. Tarn seems to be offering us a deal."

"You'd be coming along with me, Grandpa?"

"If the doctor has no objection."

Tarn looked perplexed, but only for an instant. "We'd be glad to see you both over at Fabricon. You have my card. Why don't you just get my secretary to set it up? I want your visit to be a very special one."

The scientist was already on his feet. "Now if you'll excuse me, I still have a busy afternoon ahead of me."

He reached for his hat, pressing his fingers together so that tiny flecks of sugar scattered over the table.

They shook hands. Dr. Tarn gave Tom a last penetrating look. He smiled and turned away.

No sooner had the door of the diner slammed shut than Tom pounced on his grandfather: "What do you think? Is he on the level or not? And what are we going to do?"

His grandfather pushed some dark tobacco into his pipe bowl, hesitated, and then moved slowly to the window. Tom followed him anxiously. They stood watching the scientist climb into his blue convertible.

"I dunno, I really don't know," Jack mused. "He may believe what he says — or he may be spouting a line. Did you like the man?"

"No, I didn't. He was impressive, almost. Cool. I guess I didn't dislike him as much as I thought I would."

His grandfather nodded. "That's the way with these characters. But what ideas! You know something, Tom? I think the guy's clean out of his mind. A real nut and at the same time very clever. The most dangerous type of beast on earth."

CHAPTER EIGHT

Questions in the Dark

"More pizza, Tom?" his mother asked.

"Sure, thanks. I didn't know you were going to make it yourself, Mom. ... But don't you want any?"

She laughed. "I have to think of my waistline! Here, give me your plate. I'll grab a piece from the kitchen for you."

They had been sitting in the living room watching the six o'clock news together, and now, with the sound turned off, Tom was flipping channels aimlessly, up and down, back and forth, past the same scenes and faces. The two portable fans donated by Chuck Reichert made it cooler, he had to admit, yet he regarded them with scorn just because they reminded him of the man himself.

Of course he was glad his mother wouldn't be alone so much in the apartment and that she had someone to drive her home every day. The mysterious phone calls, the fact that the man in black might be watching the place, the whole crazy thing with Fabricon — he felt bad about not telling her to be careful, but it would have meant a ton of questions. Since neither he nor grandpa had answers, the questions raised would only make his mother worry out of all proportion.

"I suppose we could have a glass of wine together," she called out from kitchen. "It's not legal, but I'm sure you taste the stuff now and then."

This was what Tom thought of as a leading statement.

The occasions when, at his mother's suggestion, they did something together always had a downside. He appreciated her effort to keep in touch with him; he liked being with her and he respected her intelligence. But at the same time he knew that she would only be happy if she thought he was telling her everything: his real thoughts and fears and hopes, what was happening in his world and among his friends.

How could he tell her what was happening among his friends? He didn't go to the parties (and wouldn't be going tonight, either) and he heard the crazy stuff mostly second-hand when he played pool with Pete or went for bike rides with Bim.

Did his mother really want to hear that Kim Baker had gone the limit with two boys together in the back of her car last month? That Charlie Allison, stoned out of his mind, had fallen into the river and nearly drowned? That Nat Spivack was ripping off stereos in the suburbs? That two guys on the football team beat up Jim Fossi because they thought he was gay?

Such things happened all the time, but Tom was pretty sure they weren't what she wanted to hear.

And how could he tell her what was in his own mind (it seemed a horrible thing to have to do, anyway) when his feelings soared and sank without warning or cause, when his hopes shifted and changed every week, when his fears centred on things he knew were crazy but couldn't help wondering about anyway.

He didn't want his mother around when he stood in front of the mirror, trying to figure out who he was, worrying about every change in his face and body — the sprouting hair, the pimples, the bags under his eyes. He was always replaying the same questions in his mind. Was he a freak or just like everyone else? Could he make it with girls? Would he be famous and rich? Would he travel around to places like Paris and London and be respected and as cool as anyone?

If he talked about such things with his mother he knew she would look at him intently and say in her quiet voice, "I'm sure that you can do whatever you set out to do, Tom. If you only work hard enough and don't lose confidence in yourself."

She might say that, but she would never say, "It might have happened. You might have achieved anything if that father of yours had stuck around and paid a few of the bills."

How could he tell her what was bothering him now? While they were walking home from Damato's his grandfather had reminded him that it was too soon to say a thing.

"We've got to do some work," he'd insisted. "We've got to start asking questions. When we go over to

Fabricon we should know a whole lot more than we know now. You've got to talk to your friends, get some evidence of … whatever's happening. And we've got to challenge that watcher fella. All that highfalutin' talk from Tarn and he's got some goon spying on us!"

Tom's mother appeared from the kitchen, put the pizza slice and the wine on the little table in front of him, and gently reached out to take the remote from his hands.

He pulled it away from her, too roughly, and she protested.

Suddenly he felt terrible. He flipped off the set and handed her the instrument.

"I'm just fed up with staring at that silly box," she said, and tossed the remote at nearby chair. Her aim was poor and the instrument clattered on the floor. The batteries popped out and rolled away.

Tom jumped up to collect them. "Good shot, Mom," he said, and they laughed together.

There was a knock at the door, and he clutched the batteries tightly in his hand.

"I'll get it, Mom."

He opened the door with some trepidation and frowned at the figure standing there.

It was Bim Bavasi, wearing a jacket, a maroon turtleneck, and fresh jeans. His dark hair was cut in a new way, a bit fussy and artificial, and his hands were busy with a cigarette.

Tom, a little taken aback, blustered, "Bim! Great to see you. I got your note."

"So? You ready to go?"

"Go where?"

"The party, stupid! I'm supposed to pick you up."

"Who said that?"

"Estella. She told me you'd go if I picked you up."

"I never said I'd go."

"Who's that at the door?" his mother called out. She came around the chairs, carrying her wine glass, and nodded to Bim.

"Why don't you invite your friend in?"

Tom saw Bim's look, the young male sizing up an older woman, taking in her dress and figure, and a black anger seized him.

"I'll call you tomorrow," he said and shoved at the door.

"Hey! Wait a minute!" Bim stuck his foot out and blocked it. "I heard about your trip to Fabricon. Were you stoned or something? What the hell's going on?"

"I'll talk to you tomorrow."

"What's the matter with you? There's a celebration. A real party this time. Everybody's coming. Even Maggie Stevenson. You mean you're going to pass up an evening with those fabulous breasts?"

"Shut up, will you!" Tom felt his face flare red. "I'll call you tomorrow, Bim. I gotta go now."

His friend took a step back. He shrugged his shoulders, his dark eyes glittered, his face twisted into a smile that was partially a sneer. *Smoking up*, Tom thought. And the guy has to come here!

He shut the door quickly. He wished to hell Bim had stayed in the country.

"Was that Bim Bavasi?" his mother called out to him. She had filled up her wine glass and was sitting on the couch, not looking at him at all. "I don't know why you can't invite your friends in."

She went on in a low voice, still not looking at him, as he tried to slip past her, sliding around the couch toward the safety of his room.

"We don't have much of a place, I guess, but they *are* your friends. When I was a kid we didn't care so much about those things. ... I thought Bim looked so nice in that jacket. I wish you'd dress up sometimes, Tom. You'd look so great in that cashmere your grandfather bought you. Don't you ever want to go to the parties? God! Those college parties! I used to love them. The engineers used to come over from Tech. I would end up dancing on the tables ... Of course we were a bit older."

"I'm going out for a walk, Mom." He thought if he stayed there a minute longer he'd suffocate.

"But you haven't finished your pizza. And I thought we were going to have a glass of wine together."

"You keep the pizza hot, Mom. I got some money today and I'm dying to get the new *Heavy Metal*. Don't worry, I'll be right back."

He shoved his feet clumsily into his battered old running shoes and got away before his mother could say another word.

The street seemed warm and, after the steady roar of the fans, almost silent. He looked up at the lighted window of their apartment and imagined his mother sitting there, worrying about him, about his future. He felt like a rat for running out on her, but he couldn't stand the hassle. And he could have killed Bim for coming over. Why wouldn't they let him be? He didn't always want to hang out — least of all now, when he needed time to think, to figure out his next move.

He wondered if life would have been any easier if his dad had stuck around. There were quite a few things he couldn't talk to his mom about. Maybe with his dad it would be different. But then Joe Blake obviously wasn't interested; otherwise why had he stayed away all these years? Why hadn't he ever gotten in touch with them? His mother hadn't made it easy, of course, but there were ways his dad could get through to him without stirring her up. Yet he had never bothered. Tom wondered what he would do if his dad made the attempt. Receive him with open arms? Walk away in disgust?

Nesrallah's candy store was two blocks away. He hustled along and was there in a few minutes. A couple of ten-year-olds were frigging around with one of the game machines; otherwise the place was empty. Tom couldn't find the magazine, and he knew it was no good asking Nesrallah. You would have to nuke him to get him off his butt. Since nobody was around he stood looking at a few of the girlie mags, awestruck by the images he saw within. After a while Nesrallah shouted over, breaking into his dream, "Hey! Put them back or buy them. I'm not running a strip tease!"

"I'm looking for *Heavy Metal*, Nes!"

"It's already gone. Tuesdays, I told you, or else it's gone. Get your nose out of those magazines! Whatsamatter, you can't find a real girl?"

Tom swore, but under his breath. Nesrallah could get abusive and it was no good antagonizing him. He put the magazines back and walked coldly past the storekeeper.

"In a few years you'll have one for yourself," Nesrallah said, unsmiling, without looking up from his newspaper.

Outside, it was steaming. Even the candy store's tinny air conditioning had seemed like an escape. Reichert and his portable fans! The cheap bastard — he probably got them at a discount. Tom didn't want to go back to the apartment, but he felt sorry for his mother. She was so out of it and she tried so hard.

He walked along toward the first traffic light. On his right a vacant lot, full of rubble and shadows, lay beneath the wreck of a half-demolished building. Lights glinted on broken glass and cans, and on the metal garbage shafts attached to the upper floors like fat robotic arms.

In the lot, wrapped in shadows, he saw the shape of a car. It was facing right toward him, and as he came up to it, he could hear the engine running quietly. Suddenly the headlights flashed on, blinding him. A man's head appeared at the driver's window.

"I'll turn the lights out," a voice said. "But don't try to run. Just stand right there and listen. I'm not going to hurt you. Do you hear me, kid?"

Tom recognized the voice at once. This was the moment his grandfather had warned him about! Nothing would take him into that lot, but he stopped in his tracks, blinking in the bright light. The man might run him down if he moved.

Abruptly, the headlights went out.

"Don't look at me," the man whispered. "Just lean on the front of the car, as if you were waiting for someone. If a car comes by and notices you, step back here. I have to ask you a few questions."

"Who are you?" Tom whispered, looking off down the street. Some cars cruised by the traffic lights, but the nearest pedestrian was blocks away. "Why in hell are you following me? I could report this to Dr. Tarn."

"You don't work for Dr. Tarn. You were watching Fabricon. Why?"

"No — no reason. I was just curious. I told Dr. Tarn I didn't mean any harm. Who are you? You shouldn't be following me."

"What do you know about the firm? Did your friends tell you something that scared you? Is that why you went in there? Tell me what you know."

"I went in there because I was scared of you! I don't know anything. I didn't mean to cause any harm."

"Why were they after you? Why did you run away from them?"

"I was scared."

"Are you scared of everything, kid? I don't think so. Now talk straight to me. What did Tarn tell you this afternoon? I was watching. I saw him go in there."

"He talked about the future and how helpless people are and how computers would take over the world. Stuff like that."

The man's quiet laughter seemed to mock everything: Fabricon, Dr. Tarn, the whole idea of the future. Tom looked around at the garbage, the broken bottles, the metal tunnels clinging to the buildings. The dark figure in the car seemed part of all that — something cast aside and yet resilient.

"So that's what he talked about, was it? And it all made sense to you?"

Tom was about to say that he didn't like Tarn at all; he wanted to quote his grandfather's scornful phrase about the scientist being a "dangerous beast," but he was afraid this man would kill him on the spot.

"Some of it sounded weird, like that stuff about the soul being nothing and the brain being a meat machine."

There was a moment's silence. Tom turned slowly, but the figure was still there, a dark shape in the front of the vehicle.

"Listen, I have to get back to my mother. Why are you following me? I'm going over there — to Fabricon — with my grandfather. Don't you know that?"

Still the man was silent. Tom took a step toward him.

"Listen to me, kid. I'll leave you alone, but there are two things I have to tell you. If you listen carefully and cooperate, you won't have any trouble from me. Come just a little closer and pay attention."

Tom took a step closer.

"When you go over to Fabricon, watch out for the Pavlov Room. You got that? The Pavlov Room. Stay away from there, whatever you do. You understand? The second thing is: don't mention me at Fabricon. If you do, you may never get out of there alive. As far as you're concerned, I don't exist. You understand that?"

Tom swallowed hard and nodded. "Yeah, I understand."

"I'm coming back to see you after you pay your visit. So keep your eyes and ears open. I need whatever information you can give me. But keep your mouth shut about this meeting. Now get the hell out of here!"

The headlights flashed on; the car engine roared. Tom ducked away, jumped over a castaway tire, and sprinted down the street.

He was so agitated it was hard to think straight. But a few things seemed to be coming clear.

He doesn't work for Fabricon. Otherwise, why would he warn me, why would he tell me to keep quiet? Unless it's some kind of trick ... a set-up, some kind of set-up.

Tom desperately needed to talk to his grandfather. He considered hiking over there at once, but that would mean running out on his mother. It was their evening together and he just couldn't do it. He would have to go back and eat pizza and act as if nothing had happened.

He took the apartment stairs two at a time. On the landing he could already smell the hot pizza, and he heard his mother's laughter through the thin walls. He stopped right there and thought *Reichert*, but it wasn't Reichert.

Pushing the door open, he made her jump. She smiled, however, and stepped back and spoke into the telephone.

"He's here now."

She handed him the phone. "Grandpa," she explained, and rushed off to the kitchen.

He heard the rattle of pans on the counter, his mother humming to herself. She sounded happy.

"Tom!" Jack croaked at him. "He's been here! The guy who was watching you."

"When?"

"About an hour ago. He drove me over to Fabricon and dropped me off back here."

"I saw him a few minutes ago."

"He didn't tell me he was going there. He must have wanted to talk to us separately. What did he say?"

"He asked a lot of questions."

"We've got to talk. Can't trust the phones. Can you meet me somewhere?"

"Sure. But not tonight. Mom and I are having pizza."

"So she said. … OK. The comic book store, then, tomorrow at about ten. Call me if anything comes up."

"Right."

His grandfather rang off. Tom stood holding the phone.

"Pizza and wine in the café," shouted his mother from the living room.

CHAPTER NINE

Humiliation

The next morning, Tom slept in. Vaguely, he heard his mother call out a goodbye, then the door slammed and the roar of the fans filled up the morning silence — she must have turned them on as she left the apartment.

Wrapped in sweaty bedsheets, he fought off dreams of being trapped in swamps and of standing stripped naked in front of his high school class. Sleep became impossible and he got up, only to find that he was late for the meeting with his grandfather.

He splashed water in his face, threw on some clothes, and left the apartment, a piece of cold pizza in one hand and a small can of orange juice in the other.

Crosstown Comics, on the other side of Pitt Park, was one of the surviving concerns in a cheap, half-deserted mall that had once featured a dry cleaner, a small hardware store, and a porno shop. Although a new chain had recently moved into town, as far as Tom's grandfather was concerned Crosstown Comics was the place of choice.

Tom got there at ten-thirty but Jack Sandalls was nowhere to be seen. The boy bought a pastry in the tiny coffee shop at one end of the joyless mall and walked around, eating it slowly, watching the lethargic traffic and waiting for the comics store to open.

The store was a hole-in-the-wall operation run by an ex-hippie named Sebastian, who lived upstairs in the space behind the fire escape and a few withered plants. Crosstown's greasy windows were posted up with crude, hand-lettered sale signs that never changed, while inside there was barely room to turn round. The place was crammed with magazines and comics of all kinds, old LPs, and tapes. It stank of smoke and incense, and some said you could get high just by hanging out there for ten minutes, but Sebastian was a cheerful owl-like presence who sold everything at a reasonable price and knew a lot about comics. If you pressed him he would begin to talk about the good old days in Haight-Ashbury.

Minutes passed, but there was no sign of Jack. After the morning rush, the city seemed to be afflicted with a deep uncertainty, as if its frenzy of devotion to duty had been snuffed out by the heat. Tom was beginning to worry a little about his grandfather; he half-expected a pickup to drive out of the distant park and a grim driver to lean out the window and order him inside. Yet what had happened last night affected him like a persistent nightmare that has suddenly developed a good side. The man was scary, but it was just possible he wasn't working for Fabricon — unless his advice and questions were part of some weird plot by Dr. Tarn.

Why did things have to be so complicated? It was hard to know who to trust, who to rely on — and Tom wondered if that was something you learned in the big world, or an instinct you were born with that got you through safely where others faltered. Strangely enough, he felt that he might be able to trust the man in black, whereas he would never trust Chuck Reichert at all — those were just his instincts, all he had to go on, and he might be crazy to follow them.

He peered down the street and had just reached a desperate pitch of restlessness when he saw his grandfather appear in the distance, a rotund figure in a battered golf hat and sunglasses, swaying along on an old ten-speed. When he came close enough to shout a greeting, easing his bike up the broken ramp beside a long-vanished hamburger concession, all Tom's worries seemed to float away like dust in the morning sunlight.

"Don't tell me that Sebastian isn't up yet!" Jack muttered, locking up his bike in front of Crosstown's smeary windows. "Well, it's another damned muggy morning. Had some trouble dragging myself out of bed and into action. Didn't want to face the day at all — longing for a nice sea breeze in all this heavy weather!"

Pulling his sunglasses off, he gave Tom a sharp look.

"You OK, son? Your mom OK? We've got to talk! Things are breaking a little too fast for my liking."

They went together to find a table in the coffee shop. A waitress in a soiled apron took their order for coffee and juice without even looking at them. Tom told his grandfather the details of his encounter of the previous night and the old man slowly lit up his pipe.

"So he gave you something like the same yarn, did he?" Jack nodded. "That man is quick. And he's handed us plenty to think about. Can we trust him, Tom?"

"I don't know, Grandpa. He warned me about the Pavlov Room, a place I should stay away from. The guy seems weird, pretty scary, and he wants us to give him information. But you know, when I really believed him was when he laughed at Tarn's ideas."

"What do you mean?"

"He asked me what Tarn said to us, and when I told him he laughed. But it wasn't an ordinary laugh. It was a deep kind of scornful laugh, as if he could never believe anything that Tarn predicted about the future."

Jack considered this. He sipped his coffee and leaned forward. "Now, listen, Tom. We're at a disadvantage in this game because we don't know anything about anybody. We need to get filled in a bit better before we see Tarn. There's a couple of things I want you to do for me."

"OK."

"Call Tarn's office and make our appointment, but don't make it tomorrow, no matter what they say. There's another thing — you've had a pretty good look at that fella by now, even if it was dark or on the run. As soon as you get home I want you to draw me the best picture of him you can."

Tom shook his head. "You know I'm not an artist, Grandpa."

"Look, don't play games with me! You're good enough to do me a sketch. I need a sketch to do some checking on this fella, understand? And you're the only one who can do it."

Tom nodded doubtfully. He felt under pressure, but he couldn't say no to his grandfather.

"You've still got the sketch pad and stuff I gave you?"

"Yeah …"

"I know a few people who might be able to help me find out who this fella is. I also want to see if I can get hold of the Fabricon company reports and to check the newspapers for interesting stuff. So we need some time, a couple of days. We can't go to see Tarn before Monday at the earliest."

"What do I tell the kids in the meantime? They're bound to ask questions."

"Don't tell them a thing! Try to pretend what you did was a lark. Brush it off. But get as much from them as you can. You know what I figure?"

"What?"

"I figure we know a few things. It looks like Tarn does have something to hide. It's also possible that some kind of indoctrination is going on over there. It also looks like Tarn and the boys have an enemy who's watching them and looking out for ways to get at them. You know who Pavlov was, Tom?"

"Some kind of scientist, right?"

"A scientist who worked out conditioned reflex-es. You know, stimulus and response stuff. You ring a bell every time you feed the dog, then pretty soon when you ring the bell the dog salivates, food or no food."

"Is that important, Grandpa?"

"It's important because what you saw might have been some kind of conditioning. If there was a worse kind of conditioning going on, where do you think it might happen?"

Tom looked at his grandfather. "In the Pavlov Room?"

Jack smiled. "Bright fella!"

They finished up the coffee and juice; Jack threw some change on the table.

"I'm going to pass up the comics this morning. I've got too many things to check out," he explained, as they emerged from the dingy cafe into the sunlight. "If I don't die of a heat stroke I'll expect you to bring me that sketch over later." Mopping his brow, he added, "In fact, it might be a good idea to do it before your mother gets home. She doesn't know anything about this, I hope."

"No, she doesn't."

"Well, keep it that way. We'll tell her as soon as we know more. She might have some good ideas — and anyway, she has to know eventually."

Jack climbed on his bike. "Call me right away if that fella shows up again, although he said he wouldn't and I somehow believe him."

Tom waved as his grandfather pedalled away. The old man, wobbling a little, picked up speed and began to cruise bravely among the light mid-morning traffic.

Tom glanced at the comic book shop. Sebastian had shoved the door half-open and was struggling to haul out some cases full of LPs for a sidewalk display, smiling wryly at his own clumsiness and muttering to himself as he did so.

Tom ambled over to help and Sebastian thanked him. "Coming in?" he asked, wiping his forehead and his grey mop of hair with an old dishtowel. "I see Jack's gone already."

"Yeah."

Tom didn't feel like looking at magazines this morning, but he didn't want to disappoint Sebastian, either. Some days customers were pretty scarce at Crosstown, so for a while he poked around among some copies of *Heavy Metal*, trying to find one he could buy, while Sebastian opened boxes and put on an old Pink Floyd album. A ceiling fan slowly revolved, doing little to cool the place, and Tom was just getting ready to move along when, much to his surprise, a bright red Camaro screeched up and stopped outside the store.

Two teenage hunks in cut-off jeans and a stunningly pretty blonde girl got out, laughing and playfully shoving at one another. The girl was nearly as tall as the big-shouldered guys, but she was as slender as a dancer and moved with the same kind of easy grace. Despite the sunglasses, there was no mistaking that face; Tom recognized Maggie Stevenson immediately.

The trio drifted across the sidewalk, and he saw to his horror that they were heading straight for

Sebastian's store. He started to move, to get out of there, but his clumsy actions upset a counter display. CDs tumbled down, and while he was frantically collecting them, the door swung open and Maggie entered with her friends.

All of a sudden the place seemed about as big as a walk-in closet or a tool shed. Tom picked up the last of the CDs and took a step toward the door.

Maggie swung her hips, twirled her sunglasses in one hand, looked at him, and laughed. The hunks — they were high school football players, and one of them he remembered was named Jeff — wore expressions of smug impenetrability. *Don't look at me*, they seemed to say. *If I want your attention I'll ask for it.* It was only when they exchanged glances with Maggie that they dissolved into smirking non-resistance: if she had even so much as stuck her tongue out, it seemed, they would have melted away into Sebastian's dusty carpet.

"Morning, you guys," Sebastian greeted them. He was warming up a can of soup on a Bunsen burner.

The boys grunted but didn't deign to look at him. Maggie ignored the greeting and said, "God, it stinks in here!"

Sebastian treated this remark as if it were a piece of ordinary social discourse. "Haven't seen you guys in a while," he said. "Looking for something special?"

The hunk named Jeff elbowed the other one and guffawed.

"Seems like he's hidden the stash already, Pudge. Didn't know we were coming, huh?"

Pudge seemed to choke on his own half-suppressed laugh. "They must have raided him again. The cops took all his bubble gum and dirty pictures."

This remark launched Maggie and the two men into gales of laughter. When this subsided there was a brief pause, and Maggie cast a look at Tom, who stood with one hand clenched on the last CD he had retrieved from the floor.

"Look who's here," she said, "the Fabricon kid!"

More laughter. Tom tried half-heartedly to join in. He wondered how he could get past them and out the door. The grim shopping mall outside looked like paradise.

Maggie drifted toward him; the curve of her white T-shirt and the flash of skin at her thighs made him feel a little weak and at the same time stupidly happy. He tried not to look at her.

"Hey, he's smiling!" Pudge said. "He's been smoking up with Sebastian."

"You shouldn't do stuff like that," Maggie said. She stood so close now he could almost feel the warmth of her body — at the same time she was miles away. "You know it's bad for the complexion."

Tom blushed. He cursed the acne that had pitted and marked his cheeks and neck. His mother claimed it was better now, but that was just his mother.

"He doesn't have any complexion," Jeff said. "He's a robot. Old Dr. Tarn turned him into a robot."

Another gust of laughter. Before it had quite subsided, Maggie said quietly, "A robot with a face only a mother could love."

Tom couldn't believe what he'd heard. Full of hatred and pain, he found he could hardly swallow, hardly move his lips.

"You shut up," he managed, but his voice broke.

The jocks stared at him; they seemed to be waiting for a signal from the girl.

He felt Maggie's smile like a searchlight. "Touchy, isn't he?"

"Touchy but not feely," Jeff murmured.

"Were you buying something?" Maggie asked, reaching for the CD he still clutched tightly in his left hand. He pulled it away quickly and murmured, "I wasn't buying anything."

The jock named Pudge stepped forward and held out his beefy hand. "Let's see it," he said, in a serious voice.

Tom handed him the CD. Pudge read the label slowly: "*Overcoming Jealousy Through Self-hypnosis ...*?" He looked baffled, as if making a joke about this was a little beyond him.

"Maybe he's jealous of his mother's boyfriends," Jeff said, a wild shot that found its mark.

The laughter that followed, however, was a bit mechanical, as if they had exhausted the subject. Pudge tossed the CD onto the counter. Maggie yawned.

"I thought we came here to get that Smash and Grab poster?" she said, turning her back on Tom. Smash and Grab was a rock group; Tom hated their headbanger music. He wondered how he could get out of the shop; the three of them were still blocking his way and paying him a kind of subliminal attention, as if he were a call on hold.

"Smash and Grab — I sold that one yesterday," Sebastian said, looking up from his soup. He had seemed to be invisible, to shrink away, while they picked at Tom. "You might try The Green Dragon over on Market. They seem to have just about everything."

The Green Dragon was part of a comics chain, a bright, spacious, and well-stocked store that would have driven Sebastian out of business, if he had been a businessman in the first place.

"Shit! And we wasted our time coming here!" Maggie said.

"So what are we hanging around for?" Pudge wondered.

"Not because we like robot face," Jeff decided.

They looked at Tom without seeing him. The two jocks turned and moved lumberingly toward the door. Maggie danced after them, as if annoyed that they had dared to move without a signal from her.

"Come on, you jerks, wait up! I might trip over a dust bunny and fall on my face."

"Don't worry, we'll give you restitution," Pudge said, groping for the right word.

Tom stood still, breathing deeply. He could have shouted for joy. They were really going.

The door swung open, then shut, and he was alone with Sebastian. He watched his three persecutors as they jostled around on the sidewalk. He prayed that they would climb into the car and go, that no wayward impulse would pull them back in his direction.

"They're not very nice people," Sebastian said. He had finished his soup and was wiping the corners of his mouth carefully with a paper towel.

Tom nodded; he was too upset to say anything. The bastards were climbing into the car now, and if he could have snapped his fingers and killed them he wouldn't have hesitated.

"As a matter of fact I do have that Smash and Grab poster," Sebastian went on. "I don't s'pose you want it? Give it to you for a couple of bucks. Or maybe for nothing. Your grandpa buys a lot here."

Tom shook his head. He swallowed hard to keep the tears back.

"No, thanks," he murmured, not looking at Sebastian. "I gotta go."

With his hand on the door he heard Sebastian's high-pitched voice behind him. "Don't let those folks bother you; they think they're somewhere, but they aren't anywhere, and that's what really irks them."

Tom turned and nodded gratefully at the benevolent figure bent over the counter. Sebastian began to straighten out the CDs.

Out on the sidewalk, uncertain where to go, he took small comfort from Sebastian's thought: *Maggie's already got a modelling contract and both those guys have football scholarships at good colleges. They're* already *somewhere. I'm the one who's nowhere.*

He made his way home in a kind of daze, wondering if he could ever get his life together.

CHAPTER TEN

The Porthole Opens

Tom lay on his bed, hardly able to move. Coming back to the stifling apartment he had turned off the portable fans, and now he was sweating miserably, staring at the blotchy ceiling and the grim walls, but determined to make do without Reichert's gifts.

He knew he should be working on that drawing his grandfather had asked him for, but even though the stranger's face was clear in his mind, Tom still wasn't sure he had the skill to get it down on paper.

In fact, he wasn't feeling any too good about himself. Maggie's poisonous words had stuck with him. Arriving home, he had twisted around in front of the bathroom mirror, trying to get a better view of his face and neck. He remembered those terrible months, a couple of years ago, when acne had struck and nearly disfigured him. His grandfather had taken him to a specialist and the heavy drugs had done their job. He knew he was looking better now, but the habits formed then hadn't died. The affliction had made him shy away from people, just as he had when his father had left them and the kids began to ask embarrassing questions.

It seemed that every once in a while, whenever he felt strong enough to get his life in motion, something would happen and he would have to crawl back into his room, pull the shades down, and sit, with gritted teeth, waiting for things to improve.

All this summer he had felt much better — had almost forgotten his troubles, only to find himself left behind while all the kids flocked to join Fabricon. His suspicions had isolated him again, and nobody but his grandfather admired him for pursuing the issue.

Disgusted, Tom rolled over, threw his pillow at the wall, and cursed his bad luck. He couldn't sleep and he still couldn't work. He stumbled into the living room, flopped onto the couch, and turned the television on. Almost immediately, he began to sink into the lethargy that seemed to be part of staring at the small screen. Not caring what he watched, he flipped aimlessly, filling up his head with meaningless pictures, but soon he settled down to a pattern. He locked into two or three shows at once, switching channels during the ads and returning in time to watch a car chase, a fire, or a shoot-out, to wallow in some grotesque story of incest or rape, or to laugh mechanically at the hollow jokes of the sitcoms. After a while, even though he didn't feel so lonely, he began to despise himself.

When the phone rang, it was almost a relief. He glanced at the clock and saw that was nearly five-thirty.

Evening was coming on, and he'd done absolutely nothing. He was relieved to think that the day would be over soon.

He flipped off the TV, picked up the phone, and heard the voice of his grandfather barking at him: "Well, where's my drawing?"

He tried to answer, hesitated, and mumbled the words. "I — I'm just getting down to it. It was so hot I fell asleep."

"Are you OK? You don't sound very good. Listen, remember what I said. We can't do anything without that drawing."

"I know."

"Did you call Fabricon?"

"Uh, no. I thought I'd do the drawing first."

"Well, do it! Remember, no nonsense now. It doesn't have to be perfect and you don't have to be Picasso. Just put that mug's face on paper for me."

"Sure, Grandpa. Don't worry." He could almost feel his grandfather's energy coming over the phone and charging him up.

"I need it tonight. I wish you weren't taking so long. Your mother will be home any time now, won't she?"

"I know. That's why I didn't start."

"Do it right away. It will only take minutes. Bring it here after dinner."

"Sure, Grandpa."

But as soon as he hung up the phone, when the contact with his grandfather's voice was broken, Tom could feel his energy draining away again. He hadn't even thought to ask old Jack if he'd learned anything about Fabricon. Disgusted with himself, he flopped on the couch again and lay there, staring at his sketch pad and pencils. He knew he couldn't begin to sketch right now. He reached for the TV remote, fingering the buttons, and hating himself as he did so.

Suddenly, there was a knock on the door.

Tom got up slowly. He felt a rush of panic — one of the kids, the last thing he needed! He couldn't face anyone; he wouldn't open it.

He stood looking around the apartment, at the familiar battered furniture, the worn rug, at his own baby and toddler photos, glimpses of a lost past that his mother had arranged in a Woolworth's frame on the table. How could he pretend not to be there, to make himself invisible, as he longed to be? These walls seemed much too flimsy to protect him from the world out there.

There was another knock, then the muffled growl of a man's voice.

Could it be the stranger? But he'd said he wouldn't contact them before their meeting with Tarn. Could it be somebody from Fabricon?

Tom hesitated. Another knock, then a voice that he recognized. He moved quickly to the door and threw it open.

Mr. Rivera, the janitor, stood there shaking his grey, grizzled head.

"What's with it, you don't answer the door? You sleeping or something?" He wiped his forehead with the back of a gnarled hand. "Whew! It's hot in here. Why doesn't your mother buy a fan?"

Tom didn't answer. Mr. Rivera shrugged his shoulders, set his broom aside, reached into one pocket, and pulled out a small parcel wrapped in brown paper.

"This came for you ... looks like medicine. You sick or something?"

Tom shook his head. He held up the parcel: it was very light and neatly wrapped with string. Pasted on it was a company label on which his name had been carefully typed. He stared hard at the label, not quite believing his eyes when he took the company's name in.

Mr. Rivera grabbed at his broom and made his way slowly down the stairs, muttering to himself as he went. "This heat ... everybody sleeping ... misery!"

Tom cradled the parcel in his hands. The building around him seemed suddenly to shed its rough walls, its raw smells, its filth and decay. His hair stood up a bit on the back of his neck, and he felt as if he were turning in space, peering out of some secret room at a blue horizon that was infinite and yet familiar.

In tiny letters, the label on the parcel read: "MERCURY ENTERPRISES, 221 HARBOUR STREET, WEST HOPE."

Tom slammed the apartment door, raced into his bedroom, and tore the parcel open. He tossed aside the loose string and ripped paper, then opened up the small cardboard box he found inside.

A faint and delicate perfume seemed to invade the room. In the box was a piece of printed paper, stamped with a symbol he vaguely recognized — two snakes twisting around a wand. Beneath this image were some hand-printed words that seemed even more familiar but that he didn't precisely understand.

Ad astra per aspera, the words read.

Tom folded the paper carefully and hid it in one of his dresser drawers. He saw that there was something else in the box, a worn cardboard insert, clipped to which was what looked like an old-fashioned tie pin.

He pulled it out, only to find it wasn't a pin but a ring, a gold ring, cheaply made and tarnished a little, with a one-size-fits-all adjustable band. There was a small catch on one side of the ring. Tom flipped the catch and found that the inside was hollow.

He held the ring up and saw his face in the small convex mirror set inside. As he moved the ring, a few objects in the room were visible around him, but his head appeared oddly distanced and disembodied, like one of those "phantom doubles" of themselves that the heroes of fantasy stories sometimes encountered.

He was puzzled — and thrilled.

He hurried to the phone and dialled his grandfather's number. Jack answered almost immediately.

"Tom! I was expecting you. Where are you?"

"I'm still at the apartment, but I'm coming right over. I have to ask you something right away. Do you know what *ad astra per aspera* means?"

"Hang on, let me write that down. Hmmm … seems to me you should know what that one means. But if you want an exact translation of the Latin, I can look it up.

Why don't I do that and tell you when you get here? Are you coming now? Have you got the drawing?"

"I'm bringing it with me, Grandpa."

Within minutes, Tom had carefully hidden away the half-torn wrappings and the tiny printed paper with the Latin phrase. He fitted the ring to his finger, squeezing the band a little to get it tight, and then, feeling much better, he began to sketch.

His hands moved, everything seemed easy and natural, and as he worked he felt the image growing strong and sure at his fingertips. With many deft, bold strokes he slowly evoked on the white page the face of the man who had pursued him.

After a while he realized that he had finished. He held the sketch at arm's length. The stranger's intense gaze seemed to fix on him. He nodded with satisfaction, flipped the pad shut, and found his door key.

It was well after six. His mother might be home at any minute. He wanted to get out of there, and he wouldn't bother to leave a message.

Racing along Morris Street, he was thinking, *How did the ring get to me? Mercury Man Comics shut down long ago. The kids would think I've lost my mind, but I've got the ring — some kind of magic is happening. This is crazy, but at least something's happening, I'm sure of it! But who sent it? Have I found some kind of porthole at last?*

Arriving at his grandfather's, he slipped the ring in his pocket before he handed over the sketchbook and listened to Jack sing his praises.

"Now that's more like it! I wondered if you were ever going to finish it! But it's good, Tommy boy, it's damned good. I never understood why you didn't keep up with your sketching!"

Jack slapped him heartily on the back, then held the picture up once again and stared at it.

"Today I talked to a couple of old buddies down at *The Clarion*. There's a cop I know who might help, too. I'm hoping we can pinpoint this guy and find out what his game is. I'm also working on Fabricon's corporate history. You never got through to them to set up the appointment?"

"Tomorrow, for sure."

"Good! Anyway I found the translation of that Latin for you. *Ad astra per aspera*. It means, approximately, *Along rough paths to the stars*. I'm surprised you didn't remember it. Didn't you do a prize essay on that theme in first year high?"

"Oh, I remembered the essay all right, but I forgot the Latin words."

"It's what they call a tag, or saying, I guess. Means that you sometimes have to go through the mill to get a sight of something better. I always regretted I never learned any Latin. Sailed into Pireaus so many times that I picked up quite a bit of Greek, though. Hung out in a taverna or two in my time."

Jack sighed. "God! Sometimes I wish I had a deck under my feet again! I'd love to show you some of those great ports of call I used to anchor in. Hobart, Tasmania — now there's a harbour. Beats Naples any day! You're coming over here tomorrow afternoon? Good! I may have a few leads by then."

Before Tom left, though, he had one more question. He drew a picture for Captain Sandalls: a staff with crossed figures of serpents and wings at the top.

"Does that remind you of anything, Grandpa? I've seen it before in your collection, and other places, too, but I can't exactly remember what it is. I think you once told me it had something to do with the old Western Union telegraph company."

"Heck, that's an easy one. That's the staff of the Roman god Mercury. The messenger of the gods, you know. Always around when something new was about to happen. Remember the comics I showed you the other day?"

"Sure, *Mercury Man*."

"Just one of the cases where the comics used those old Roman gods. Fine fellow, Mercury — I always had a sneaking liking for that thief!"

"Thief? I thought he was supposed to be a good guy."

"Well, he was. But he didn't care how he made things happen, I guess."

Tom walked home slowly, elated by what he had heard. He needed some time to think, and the ring and the Mercury symbol were at the centre of his thoughts.

As soon as he was out of sight, he slipped the gold band back on his finger, a little ashamed of not telling his grandfather about it, but glad all the same that he hadn't. Not that the old man wouldn't have understood — it would have tickled him mightily, almost as if

Tom had literally stolen a page from one of his treasured comic books. Yet he knew, for reasons he couldn't fathom, that telling his grandfather would be a mistake. He needed to sort out his own thoughts, to figure out where the ring had come from and why its arrival made him feel suddenly happy and powerful.

When he got to his building he stopped at the ground floor and knocked on Mr. Rivera's door.

The grizzled old man stumbled into the hallway. He didn't seem very glad to see him. The air smelled of chillies and Mr. Rivera's breath reeked of booze.

"The parcel," Tom said, "thanks for bringing it up." He offered him a dollar, but the old man waved his hands violently, as if he had been mortally insulted.

"You keep your money, I don't need it. I don't have to take money from kids. Not yet, anyway!"

He seemed almost ready to spit in disgust at the thought, but then turned away abruptly, just before Tom got out his question.

"Sorry, but I wanted to know — I mean you didn't mention — did the postman bring this today?"

Mr. Rivera stopped and half-turned. He seemed puzzled by the question.

"Postman? No, no. Not postman. I don't touch postman stuff. Girl brought it. Pretty girl. She didn't say nothing." He pointed to his lips. "Maybe from drugstore, huh?"

Before disappearing into his apartment, Mr. Rivera waved his hand in the direction of the corner pharmacy, some three blocks away.

"Must be from that drugstore. I got to go now."

Tom doubted that Mr. Rivera's guess was right, though. The only pretty "girl" he had ever seen working in the drugstore was older than his mother.

But now he had at least part of the explanation, for the Mercury Man wrapper he had carefully stashed in his dresser drawer bore just the slightest odour of a delicate and unfamiliar perfume.

Ad astra per aspera, Tom thought, and climbed the stairs slowly, one by one.

CHAPTER ELEVEN

A Shocking Revelation

Tom opened his eyes, and his sweating body told him that the heat had not abated, although the sunlight suggested it was already late morning. He sensed by the hollow silence of the apartment that he was alone. It was Saturday but his mother must have gone out somewhere.

He dragged himself up and started for the bathroom, but stopped suddenly and slid open the top drawer of his small dresser. The ring was right where he had concealed it, under his spring report card. He smiled to himself — a ridiculous ring, but a real mystery — delivered by some girl and actually for him! He slipped it onto the second finger of his right hand and suddenly felt alive: life had changed, he'd been given sight of a secret — something he couldn't guess but was surely well worth exploring.

In the living room he looked around, rubbing his eyes. A sheet of paper had been pinned to the doorway:

Tom — Going out for breakfast with Chuck. Thought you might like to go with us to a softball game tomorrow. Lots of interesting people there and free eats! How about it? — Love from Mom

By the way, Dr. Tarn called from Fabricon. Sorry, I almost forgot. I was just going out the door. He wants you to call him right away. I told him you were asleep and he said call when you wake up. Didn't know you applied for a job there. Good luck!

In her usual careless way, she had scrawled a barely readable telephone number at the bottom of the paper. Tom shook his head, groaned, crumpled the note, and tossed it on the floor. His mother was priceless! Desperate for him to "do something" but not willing to wake him up when an executive called. She was so out of it! If she didn't think all the time about Reichert she might notice what was going on around her!

Tom splashed water in his face, rubbed his eyes with a towel, and stared at himself in the bathroom mirror. How was he going to handle the weekend? A series of images flashed through his mind: he saw himself at the company softball game, holding up his ring to make Reichert and the others disappear; he imagined himself and his grandfather trapped in some vault at Fabricon, only he knew that with the ring he would find the way out; he was having coffee at Damato's and a beautiful girl was quietly explaining to him why she had brought him the ring in the first place …

Water glugged slowly down the slow drain. Tom stared at the green walls, the cracked plaster of the tiny bathroom. His daydreams vanished suddenly and a terrible thought came into his mind: suppose somebody had sent him the ring as a joke? Maybe the kids were making fun of him? The only beautiful girl he knew was the disgusting Maggie!

In the morning mirror his face looked white, strained, and ugly. He hated his haircut, almost everything about himself. He felt powerless, retarded: other kids were driving cars and going to casinos and he was frigging around with crackerjack toys.

He drifted out of the bathroom and flopped on the couch. He sat there a minute, rubbing his eyes, swallowing hard, and thinking, *Everything is hopeless.* Then suddenly he realized he was starving. In the kitchen, he pulled some bread and bacon from the fridge and began, with a kind of desperation, to make himself a sandwich. The phone rang just as the toast popped and the smoking bacon had begun to crisp and darken in the pan.

Tom swore and pulled the pan off the heat.

"Dr. Tarn speaking," the voice said, after Tom had mumbled a hello. Hearing the voice he stiffened; his fingers tightened around the receiver.

"Yes, sir. … My mother said you called."

"Tom — I need you and your grandfather to come to Fabricon today. I'm sorry, but I have other engagements next week. I hope you can make it at one o'clock this afternoon?"

"But, Dr. Tarn ..."

"I don't want to be unpleasant about this, but we're doing you a favour, you may recall. We have every right to prosecute you for breaking in."

Tom pressed the receiver hard against his ear.

"I've already explained the situation to your grandfather. I believe that he'll be coming to pick you up. I just want to be sure that you wait for him."

"Yes, sir. I'm right here."

"That's excellent. See you at one o'clock then."

Tom put the receiver down slowly. The smell of bacon filled the apartment. He went into the kitchen and ate the slices from the pan, wiping his greasy fingers on his sleeping shorts.

The food seemed to quell his panic.

He tried to call his grandfather, but there was no answer. It was eleven o'clock. He warmed up the toast, buttered it, and ate it. Then he hopped into the shower, towelled himself dry, and changed into his favourite khaki pants and a green T-shirt. He slicked his hair in various unsatisfying ways, his mind racing through what seemed a million difficult questions.

The man in black had warned them about Tarn. Now Tarn was pressuring them to go over to Fabricon. They would have to be careful, very careful ...

While he was trying to decide whether or not it would be good luck to wear his ring, he heard a knock on the door and opened it to find his grandfather standing in the hallway, shifting his feet and looking uncomfortable.

"Those stairs get steeper every day," Jack mumbled, puffing a little and wiping his forehead with a large white handkerchief.

The old man was jacketless, dressed in khaki slacks and sporting a red T-shirt, decorated all over with green parrots. It seemed to Tom that he wore the expression of a reluctant truant officer.

"I see you got Tarn's message," he said, stepping inside, taking in Tom's spruced-up look, and heading straight for the kitchen. He poured himself several glasses of water, sniffed at the bacon smells, and wiped his face repeatedly with the handkerchief.

"He called me, too — this is damned sudden! I wonder why he's pressuring us right now? I have an eerie feeling he might have guessed I'm checking up on him — or else he assumed I would. Remember what the man in black told us?"

"To watch out for the Pavlov Room."

"Right! And we will. Now let's get out of here and plan our strategy in a cooler place."

Tom ducked into his bedroom, took off his ring, and shoved it back in his dresser drawer. He locked the apartment and they walked along Morris Street toward the Hollis intersection. Tom was relieved to see that no one was around. Could his friends be going to that company softball game tomorrow? In that case they would see his mother with Reichert.

"What's the matter, pal? You don't want to let Tarn

get you down. I don't think he's going to try to brain-wash us in broad daylight, do you? We have to keep our eyes and ears open, that's all."

Jack laughed, coughed a little, and reached into his pocket for his pipe.

They turned down Hollis and walked toward the harbour.

"It's not that, Grandpa ..." Tom took a deep breath and fixed his gaze on the traffic lined up in the direction of Market Square. "I wanted to ask you ... Do you think ... Do you think my mother's going to marry Chuck Reichert?"

Jack cleared his throat but didn't answer. They kept on walking. The old man struck a match on his finger-nail and got his pipe alight. Tom felt his glance come around slowly.

"She hasn't talked to me about it, son. You don't like Chuck very much, do you?"

Tom didn't look at his grandfather. He kept his eyes on a delivery truck from which two men were unloading cases of soda water. "He's an idiot. I can't stand the guy. I'm moving out if he hangs around much longer."

"Well, I can't say he's the catch of the season — but there are worse fish in the pond. Anyway, you have to keep your cool about it. Your mom has a right to lead her own life. She's taken good care of you for a long time. You ought to give her credit for having some good instincts."

"She's just taken in by that guy! Girls and women sometimes go for guys who are totally creepy, Grandpa, you know that!"

Jack guffawed so loudly that a few shoppers turned in their direction.

"Well, I know a few ladies who've gone for me, and that sure wasn't smart! I wouldn't underestimate any gal's instincts when it comes to relationships, son. Even their mistakes sometimes have a side to them that makes us guys look like fools and innocents. When you've got one of your own you'll find out all right!"

Tom felt a kind of fury boiling up inside him. He couldn't stand it when his mother or grandfather referred to his potential wife or girlfriend. It was as if they were trespassing on the most secret territory of his imagination.

He shoved his hands in his pockets, bent his head toward the pavement, and refused to look at his grandfather all the rest of the way.

The Fabricon building loomed above them down Harbour Street. Tom was painfully aware of its sunlit tower, reaching up into the blue noon sky. So here was the scene of his crazy antics of a few days before! Fabricon seemed the end point of a series of mistakes, the miserable conclusion to his life in that claustrophobic apartment, where his father had left them to the mercy of people like Reichert.

They stopped in the little park opposite the company building. It was the place where Tom had first seen the man in black, but today it seemed pleasantly busy, transparent, and innocent. Two shirt-sleeved men occupied one of the large street benches near the bus stop — they might have been on a lunch break from Fabricon.

Jack bought hot dogs and soft drinks from a vendor who had parked his cart at the fountain, then led the way to a seat underneath the tall poplars that enclosed the place at the rear.

"Don't talk too loud here," the old man cautioned. Tom didn't want to talk at all; he was busy gulping the delicious food. Not far away, a couple of women had parked their strollers; they sat smoking, in close conversation, watching three small children who were playing in the sandbox beside them.

When they had finished the hot dogs and had ice cream to boot, Jack lit up his pipe again, looked around the park, and explained, "We have to go in there and I still haven't got the dope I need. But here's the game. We stick together. We avoid the Pavlov Room. We don't breathe a word about our friend in black. After we get out we can compare notes. This should fulfil your obligation to Tarn, and it wouldn't hurt if you seem to be — if we both seem to be — much happier about Fabricon when we walk out that door. Any questions?"

"No, Grandpa."

"Hell, then, let's go!"

They crossed the street, pushed through the doors and into the building. Standing in the silent, brightly lit foyer Tom sensed at once that the place was relatively deserted — it was Saturday, after all, and even Fabricon must cut back a little on the weekend. Was that why Tarn had wanted them today?

They walked around the fountain and found the reception desk occupied by a slender woman wearing a white lab jacket. She was giving most of her attention to a high-powered laptop and only slowly looked up at them through her shaded horn-rimmed glasses. Tom wasn't sure, but he thought he might have seen her on his earlier visit — he didn't remember the glasses, though.

"We have an appointment with Dr. Tarn," Jack told her and gave her their names.

She nodded, picked up the phone, and dialled a number.

"Dr. Tarn is on his way down," she said. She turned her attention back to the computer.

Minutes later, Tarn appeared at the inner door. He too was wearing a white lab jacket; his high-polished shoes clicked slightly on the corridor floor. He greeted them with a smile and a sharp blue-eyed glance that seemed to have more amusement than malice in it.

"So glad you could make it. Thanks very much, Marie," he said, and led them into the bland hallway that Tom remembered vividly, as if from a nightmare or a past life. Yet everything seemed relaxed and easy and his grandfather winked reassuringly as they followed the scientist into the inner recesses of Fabricon.

Tarn led them straight into a spacious room, furnished with leather chairs and a sofa, expensive lamps, a huge carved table, oriental rugs, and a battery of sophisticated but elegant equipment. Fax machines, telephone, computers, monitors, and printers — all seemed to have been specially designed in matching dark green and black decor for that setting.

Tarn pointed them to seats on the sofa. A door opened and a man dressed in a suit and tie pushed out a cart loaded with coffee, pastries, and soft drinks.

"Thanks, Charles," Tarn said, pouring a coffee for himself and selecting a Danish pastry. He indicated that they should help themselves, and patiently sipped his coffee while they did so.

When they had settled down, Tarn said, "I've brought you here to tell you that your little intrusion is forgiven, Tom. As I explained to you when we met, we operate this company according to the highest ideals. We're not a corporation that's indifferent to pressing social needs, and although we have a vision of the future, I'm not Dr. Frankenstein. I would like to get you on our side, and to do that I'm willing to show you what kind of problems we run into at Fabricon. That's why I've asked you here."

Jack nodded amiably; Tom remembered the cynical laughter of the man in the parking lot.

"I won't repeat my comments on the Fabricon vision — I'm sure you've heard enough from me on that score." Dr. Tarn smiled and sipped his coffee. "What I've done is had some important material prepared for you. Over there" — he indicated a small table near the doorway — "you'll find two portfolios giving all the relevant facts about the company. We don't mind admitting we've made some mistakes, and you might even find some evidence of that in the material I've provided. But I think on the whole it will be reassuring."

"Well, that's just terrific," Jack said. "I'll have a good read, then. Appreciate your providing that, Dr. Tarn."

"No problem. But there's one more thing. I'd be very pleased if you both would watch a little visual presentation we've prepared for you. I think it may change your perspective on a few things."

Tom cast a sharp look at his grandfather. Conditioning by film! The Pavlov Room! But the old man was smiling and nodding at Tarn.

"We'd be very pleased to take a look," he said.

"Good! I'll have Marie hold the portfolios at the reception desk for you. Just follow me and I think you'll see something that will begin to help you understand some of Fabricon's corporate problems. Might even induce our young friend here to join the enterprise!"

Tarn laughed and gently patted Tom's shoulder. The boy took a deep breath and forced a smile. As Tarn led the way into the corridor, Jack gave him the high sign: everything is cool, his gesture seemed to say. Tom gritted his teeth and obediently followed Tarn toward the rear of the building.

A small elevator carried them up and into the heart of Fabricon. As they stepped out, Tom saw the robot sculpture, suspended above them like a parade balloon. He recognized the lounge space, with its chairs, tables, and magazines; directly above was the balcony that had given him access to the projection area.

Tarn led them across a carpeted space, then through heavy double doors, which swung inward as they entered. A brass plate identified this as Copernicus Hall.

They were being taken to the very place where he had seen his friends being conditioned!

I should have brought my ring, Tom thought. *The ring would have protected me.*

One part of Tom's mind saw this as a joke, or as pure superstition, yet his gut feeling was very different. The world was a strange place, full of fears and uncertainties, and he hadn't yet heard of anybody with all the answers. Sometimes not even money could save you. It was better to pay your respects to fate than to be sorry later.

As they walked up the centre aisle, he looked around the auditorium. It was dimly lit, spacious, plush, beautifully contoured, and silent. Except for the three of them, it was empty. The white screen looked as pure as an operating table. Rows of curving banked seats were decorous in dark green cloth. The balconies from which he had spied on Fabricon were enclosed by a brass rail. The usual plastic fittings seemed to have been banished from this temple of luxury and quiet elegance.

"This should be just about perfect," Dr. Tarn told them, when they reached a point ten rows back from the small orchestra pit. "Why don't we sit here?"

Tom sat down warily, not daring to look at his grandfather.

"I'm going to show you one of our promo films, but I don't want you to groan over that," Dr. Tarn explained. "It's quite short and reasonably entertaining. This will be followed immediately by a special presentation, which will give you a sense of some of the problems we face. It's not something we show casually. If you have any questions afterward, I'd be happy to answer them."

Tarn signalled with his right hand; the lights dimmed and the show began on the screen above them.

"THE NEW HUMAN FUTURE," the title ran, "CODES BEYOND CHAOS." A series of colourful images flowed quickly past, figures superimposed on one another, stretched and distorted. Apelike creatures faded away into recognizable human forms; these dissolved in turn and became stiff and robotic shapes, almost threatening. The robots marched across the screen, but as they passed through a gate inscribed with the letters "FABRICON" a blue light enveloped them: each changed, transformed into a perfect human body. The human figures joined hands and danced away joyously, dissolving in a golden light at the vanishing point of a great plain.

From this point the film's narrative line became clear. It was the story of two great human accomplishments: the invention of the computer on the one hand, and the mapping of the genetic code on the other. A narrator skilfully traced these separate histories accompanied by a host of illustrations and animations. Tom sat contentedly watching. He was beginning to relax, for he could see nothing subversive in all this. He had sat through many similar films in high school and he could not believe that Tarn's film had anything to do with brainwashing. It was all very predictable and almost boring: at one point, he even had to stifle a yawn. This was nothing like what he had witnessed from the balcony on his first visit.

After a while the film began to wind down toward a conclusion. The final message was that through advanced computer techniques the individual genetic code could be mapped and dealt with. There were great benefits to come: improvements in medicine, better planning of children, a general improvement of the human family. Some dangers were casually alluded to, including the possibility of subliminal programming that would be irresistible because it was based on a map of a person's genetic inheritance. In that case, the film blithely asserted, nature itself would be doing the programming. This danger was played down, however, and the show ended with another vision of the Fabricon scientists leading the way to a brighter future.

"Very interesting," Jack commented. "A pretty good show." Tom felt greatly relieved, but the hall lights did not go up. Dr. Tarn said, "And now we have a little film that shows you one of the roadblocks we've run into in planning the future. It identifies one of the enemies of progress. We can't show this film in public, but it's quite accurate, and we hoped it might help you appreciate our problems."

Without a pause the screen lit up with a new narrative. Dr. Tarn's recorded voice boomed through the hall. Images of Fabricon floated up — its labs, its reception rooms, and the faces of its personnel, CEO Binkley prominent among them.

Then suddenly the story shifted to the question of subversion, industrial sabotage, ungrateful and corrupt employees bent on exploiting a generous company.

Tom gasped, leaned forward, and gripped the seat in front of him.

Tom felt his grandfather's grip on his arm; *steady*, it seemed to convey to him, *don't give everything away.*

Tom held his breath.

The screen had filled up with the face of the man in black.

The voice of Tarn declaimed from the screen: "This is the story of Paul Daniel, a man who betrayed Fabricon. He not only embezzled funds but stole company secrets in order to sell them to other firms. In doing so, he destroyed his own career and failed the company, his family, and his friends. His own daughter, shocked by his indictment, is now unable to speak.

"It was with sadness that our company witnessed the downfall of this brilliant man. Reluctantly, we were forced to prosecute, and Paul Daniel has now served a jail term for his crimes. As you look at these records of human failure, try to have a measure of pity for this unfortunate man."

Tom swallowed hard. The screen showed pictures and blowups of several newspaper stories. There was the man himself with his dark satanic eyebrows, his thin lips, and his twisted smile. The man they had begun to trust!

Newspaper clippings, legal documents, testimony from witnesses — the evidence piled up until it was impossible to doubt it. The film continued with words from the police: damning evidence. The man had served six months in jail and now was on probation. And there was the image of a young girl, dark-haired and lovely, looking shocked and stricken — Paul Daniel's daughter.

How could Tarn possibly be making this up? He would be sued for libel, discredited. It must be true.

A man who had betrayed his child, his family. An evil man — and suddenly Tom hated him. The very thought of him seemed to poison the air of the auditorium. Tarn had saved them from a dreadful mistake.

Tom heard his grandfather's low whistle beside him; it seemed very far away. Everything in the auditorium had faded and blurred. He swallowed hard and brushed at his eyes. Questions came to him — very many questions — but he didn't trust himself to say a word.

CHAPTER TWELVE

Welcome to the Funhouse

The taxi roared away, leaving Tom and his grandfather standing just outside the iron gate that surrounded Jack's place. Still thinking about their experience at Fabricon, they were momentarily speechless, gazing at the placid old house.

Maisie, his grandfather's particular friend, waved to them from the garden. She was wearing a colourful bandanna and a bright flowered dress, and she sang to herself as she watered her rather wilted roses.

"The life of the innocent!" Jack groaned as he looked at her, then turned abruptly to Tom. "Now listen to me. This is not going to throw us off the scent! You're not going to swallow all that Tarn stuff hook, line, and sinker, I hope!"

"How can you say that? We saw the proof right there. Tarn can't be making it up. It's Paul Daniel who's been deceiving us. No wonder he's pissed off at Fabricon!"

The taxi ride had been a torture. Tarn had ordered the cab and his grandfather insisted that they be dropped off at his place. Tom just wanted to get away.

"I saw how upset you were by the film — that's why I signalled you not to talk in the taxi. There's no telling what Fabricon can do or who works for them. We have to be very careful."

Tom shook his head. His grandfather was trying to make him feel better, and he wasn't having any of it.

"You seemed to swallow it all," the boy murmured. "You practically kissed Tarn's hand as we left. You don't have to soften the blow for me, Grandpa. I know I've been out of my mind. There's no brainwashing. Nothing bad happens in the Pavlov Room. It's all a crock. I'm going home now."

Even as he said it, he thought of Reichert lording it over his mother from the armchair and his heart sank.

Jack reached out and held him firmly by the shoulders.

"Listen to me, Tom! You thought you witnessed your friends being brainwashed. Maybe they were. And what do you think just happened to you? Paul Daniel was painted as an embezzler, but I don't think that's what got you, son."

"What do you mean?"

"Don't you think Tarn knows that your dad left you? All that stuff about Paul Daniel causing his daughter harm. Why should that come into it at all? You've been put through the wringer, Tom. Tarn knew exactly how to play it. He doesn't want you connecting with Paul Daniel at all. You've just been conditioned yourself."

Tom pulled away. The lazy Saturday traffic crawled by. Maisie's red bandanna bobbed up and down as she worked. What was his grandfather telling him? It was too fantastic.

"You have to remember. Those media guys are always manipulating us poor suckers, and Tarn is obviously working a new angle on the same old game. Why should he pass up a chance to neutralize you? You're the one who's trying to blow the whistle on him. And if he has to, he'll do it again."

Tom shook his head. This was hard to accept; his grandfather was just trying to make him feel better.

"It can't be ..."

"It *could* be, and I intend to find out if it is. I'm pushing ahead with my checkup on these people." He pointed at the Fabricon portfolios, which he had stuffed between the spokes of the iron fence. "Even their own handouts may be useful. If you don't mind I'll just take your copy along with me. I'm curious about a lot of things. For one, it's certainly odd that Paul Daniel has the same name as the guy who owns the amusement park. I can see that I've got a hell of a lot of work to do!"

Tom nodded mechanically. His body seemed to have gone numb and he found it hard to speak. Had Tarn really played with him, manipulated him?

He needed to get away. He had to think everything over. And there was something he knew he had to do.

Jack retrieved the portfolios and stood watching him.

"Are you sure you're OK?"

"I'm sure, Grandpa — and by the way, thanks."

"I'll be in touch!" Jack turned away.

Tom began a slow jog home. It felt good to have his body in motion. He didn't really want to think, but Tarn's film played in his mind. The image of that man! An embezzler! A man who had ruined his family. If Paul Daniel showed up again he would confront him. It couldn't all be just slander! Daniel would have to explain — but how *could* he explain? The world seemed to be full of liars and truth-benders — everybody changing reality around to suit himself.

Tom crossed Hollis and kept going past the pool parlour. A glance inside — a quick glance — and his pace slackened. Was that Jeff Parker in there? Jeff lounging beside the pool table, a cigarette in his mouth? It wasn't possible. Sweat streaked Tom's forehead and he brushed it away. A few days ago he wouldn't have believed it. Now he would believe anything. Or nothing.

Morris Street looked desolate; their apartment building seemed shabbier than ever. A bottle had been smashed in the dingy stairwell, and a kind of goo smeared with dirt stuck to his heels. Out of breath now and almost blinded by sweat, he entered their tiny flat — and knew in a moment it was empty.

His mother hadn't left a note this time. Tom went straight to his bedroom, pulled the shade down, and crashed on the bed. When his breathing became normal he dragged himself up, stripped down to his underwear, opened the dresser drawer, and retrieved his ring. He groaned at the futility of his dreams, slipped the ring on his finger, and lay down on the bed. The cracks in the ceiling bothered him, so he pulled the covers over his face. He tried to think, but his mind filled up with hopeless thoughts; misery seemed to have settled in for the duration. He closed his eyes. After a while, a miracle happened: he went to sleep.

He woke up in the dark and lay unmoving. The bedsheets were damp with his sweat. He stirred and threw them off. Flashing lights at the window — night outside the room. And something there, a greenish white glow as he moved his hand — his ring!

He stared at it for a while and remembered a promise he had made to himself. For some reason it seemed more important than ever to keep it. Just because of that feeling — though all the slouching demons in his soul cried "Stay!" — he dragged himself up.

Twenty minutes later he was walking by the river. His watch said nine. He headed west: there the city dwindled to insignificance between the ancient warehouses and the half-occupied factories, places full of cobwebs and lost dreams. The dying sunset, a faint smear of light on the horizon, seemed to mock West Hope itself, the city of no hope, the hub of nothing, a sad metropolis that was dwindling, moment by moment, in his mind.

Yet Tom, who had showered and changed, felt alive in his body. His blood had been stirred up by his brisk walk. Despite the confusion of things, he was taking action — amazing how that warded off the blues! He looked around at the bleak streets, the grim metal bridges, held his breath at the stink of the river. Despite a small breeze that moved flags and tattered awnings, its black sludge seemed hardly to stir.

He came out near the great pier that lay at the bottom of Harbour Street, beside a sprawl of condemned buildings. As his uncle had explained, this place had once been a centre of the river traffic. Boone Jetty, as it was called, consisted of a long wooden ramp, a few ramshackle sheds, and myriad old tires painted white and nailed to rotting posts. Nearby lay the wreck of a barge, a brown hump covered with bright green slime.

The jetty was known as a dangerous place at night — and sure enough, a couple of Camaros were zooming around, horns blasting and tires squealing as they criss-crossed paths and charged at each other. The wooden planks roared, the shacks trembled, the old tires swung on their posts. The young drivers leaned out the windows of their vehicles, swearing and threatening each other, while a couple of male bystanders laughed and calmly urinated into the river.

Tom hung back, safe in the shadows of a half-collapsed warehouse, and waited for the action to subside. When, amid a volley of vicious threats and swearing, the cars finally roared away, he slipped across the end of the jetty and cut back to the bottom of Harbour Street.

This was a curious area, some of it redeveloped and near genteel, like Water Street, from which he had last approached Fabricon — while other parts were shameless slums.

As he followed the fence away from the river he encountered not a single pedestrian, although the Fabricon tower, further up the street, rose above him like a challenge.

"Two-twenty-one," he said aloud, then murmured it again, like a mantra. "*Two-twenty-one.*" That was the place the ring had come from. He vaguely remembered a house standing between Fabricon and the amusement park, but it was a mere ghost in his mind.

He walked in that direction, however, following the high fence that enclosed the old amusement park. Above the fence loomed the roller coaster track with its single stalled car — a crazy sculpture out of a child's dream. Thanks to a few boyish incursions, he knew that behind the fence there were many buildings, in various states of decay; a house in reasonably good repair with a small garden beside it; a huge field, empty and desolate; a large shed full of old cars and equipment for long-abandoned rides and exhibits; a large pond drained of water.

Mercury House, he was sure, would be the next building. It was right next to, and in its decrepitude almost a part of, the amusement park.

He walked a little farther. An old house rose up where the long fence ended. Beyond that was a huge parking lot, a row of nondescript sheds, and then Fabricon. Everything in his life seemed pushed close together.

Two-twenty-one itself, a large clapboard structure from which the paint had long ago peeled, looked eccentric. A half-collapsed porch, unexpected dormers, and ramshackle sheds on either side made the house seem enormous.

Tom hesitated, suddenly under the spell of the place. No lights were visible, and he heard no sound — the building might have been abandoned decades ago. It was a house to breed memories and shadows.

"Two-twenty-one," he repeated. Someone had responded to his letter. The porthole had opened. A beautiful girl had arrived with the ring. And now he was going to find out who and why.

At the same time he felt uneasy. He couldn't bring himself to go right up to that door and knock. It would have been like trying to open a tomb.

He retreated and stood in the shadows beside one of the sheds. Night was falling on the city; the lights of the Fabricon tower blinked above him.

Then Tom noticed that the shed door beside him was slightly ajar. He pushed and it swung open. Pinpoints of light in the darkness — cat's eyes — and a soft purring voice.

He stepped into a small room and in the reflected street light saw piles of wood, tires, old shelves, and, comfortably settled on a huge barrel set before another door, a Siamese cat.

The cat looked benign enough, and Tom approached and stroked it. It greeted him in a plangent Siamese voice and licked his fingers. As he touched it with reassuring fingers he noticed the collar and nametag. The latter he could just barely read in the dim light. It read: "Sinbad."

"Hello, Sinbad," Tom said aloud. "What should I do now? I want to find my way to somebody mysterious."

The cat suddenly stood up on all fours, stretched its neck, licked one paw, and then jumped briskly from its perch. This motion set the barrel rocking, its metal hoop bumped against the inner door, and Tom saw at once that it, too, was open. He took a deep breath and shoved at it. It creaked and swung back. The cat seemed to have disappeared.

Tom groped in the dark and found a light switch. A dim bulb illuminated a long, dusty hall. Step by step he walked its length — at the other end another door confronted him. This one was both shut and locked.

"Dead end," he said aloud, and then noticed a small dish of milk at his feet — the cat's dish. On impulse he bent down and picked it up. Underneath lay a key. He turned the key in the lock and the door opened.

Once again he found the light switch. What a place he was in! It looked something like a mining tunnel, although boards and wooden rafters enclosed it instead of earth and rock. Metal tracks emerged from the darkness at the left and curved away into the dark tunnel as it continued to the right. On the tracks right before him sat a wheeled cart, like a roller coaster car. The vehicle was fitted out with plush leather seats and an old brass safety bar.

Without hesitation Tom climbed in and made himself comfortable in the spacious seat, securing himself in with the metal bar. This was crazy! The amusement park and the house were much closer together than he had figured.

He was just ready to climb out, to make his way back to the street, when the cat appeared at the half-open door and began to lick up milk from the bowl.

Tom grunted and called out to the cat, which looked up at him.

Then something happened — a sudden roar of machinery in the distance — and the boards of the building rattled all around him.

The cart itself began to shake, and then — with much creaking and groaning of its ancient wheels — it began to move.

Tom gasped. The cart gained speed, propelling him toward the darkness of the tunnel.

He squirmed in his seat but held on as a neon light illuminated the cobwebs above his head. A sign winked at him: "WELCOME TO THE FUNHOUSE."

The cart hurtled forward. Walls rose up and vanished; the lights flickered. Tom held on, sneezing and choking in the dust. The noise was tremendous.

He rolled around a corner. Lights flared. A figure rose out of the shadows, a black-cloaked mannequin with red eyes and a face the colour of dough. Thin hands with claw-tipped fingers groped toward him. Tom yelped and ducked away. The cart rattled onward.

He crouched behind the metal bar, hardly daring to look back. Ahead, he saw a cave like a furnace, with heat blasting out and shapes like wraiths rising in its smoky recesses. Tinny laughter sounded. Troops of demons danced in the orange light.

The cart picked up speed, bound straight for the furnace. Tom screamed. At the last minute it veered away.

He was in for it now, he thought. The tunnel stretched before him; sparks flared.

Walls slid open, and the darkness quivered with life. He saw grinning dwarves, a cave full of snakes. Skeletons glowed in gloomy recesses, giant bats swooped toward him, and three ancient crones pointed at him with crooked fingers.

It was all machinery, Tom knew, but he shuddered and ducked despite himself.

He was suddenly a child again, pursued by every terror. Sharks threatened him in the bathtub, a robot woman pretended to be his mother, a madman with an axe lurked in his parents' bedroom. He was lost in the great city, surrounded by brutal playmates eager to torture him and lock him forever in some dark place. His favourite toys were broken and cast away. He had forgotten his name.

"Stop this thing!" Tom cried aloud, but even before he had got all the words out, he felt the cart slow down. The tunnel had resolved itself into a flickering darkness. The spotlights went out and the figures faded, like dreams he was eager to forget.

Suddenly, with a clanking of metal on metal, the cart stopped. The cavelike passage was wider here, the lights brighter. He saw a dusty platform and steps leading upward.

The tracks continued, but he sprang out, fearful that the cart would start up again and that he would circle forever in that tunnel, traversing its terrors over and over only to end up where he had begun.

He stood for a moment on the platform, listening. The place was claustrophobic, full of dust and echoes, faint sounds. Something scurried in the corner and he shuddered, thinking *real rats*. He clambered up the rickety steps, leaving the tunnel behind, and pushed through a door to enter a large, brightly lit room, a place with startling white walls and a curiously ramped floor. It was disconcerting. He found he could not walk easily or even stand on the tilted floor without struggling mightily to get his balance.

Arms outstretched, he made his way forward, his stomach turning over as he tried hard not to fall on his face.

It was only a trick room, one designed to baffle the senses. But when at last he got through the doorway, it was like escaping from the gravity of another planet.

He found himself in a hall of mirrors, blinded by glittering reflections. Dozens of images of himself, weirdly stretched and changed, grimaced at him from the walls and ceiling. An impossibly fat and dumpy Tom, a Tom so thin that he threatened to disappear, a Tom with a huge head, one with giant feet, another with a disconnected head and body — their silent mockery was daunting.

He slipped quickly between the mirrors, keeping his eyes on his feet, trying not to look at the distortions of himself that moved and changed as he moved.

He opened a door and made his way along a dim passageway. Yet another door led into a deeper darkness.

A single beam of green light guided him through this place, but as he walked, streams of air blew at him, hissing in his face, ruffling his hair and clothes. It was as if he had walked into a cluster of balloons that were all deflating all at once.

He burst through the door and into the next room.

This place was like a crypt, its narrow walls glowing with reddish light. It smelled of incense — and of something else, something sickly and sweet. On one side of the room, on a high table, sat a huge black box, obviously a coffin. It was cobwebbed and dusty, carved and decorated in heavy wood, and surrounded by a few religious items — half-burned candles, a crucifix, and a rosary.

The coffin was shut. Tom remembered the waxen image of a dead childhood friend, seen long ago and in nightmares since. He realized that nothing would induce him to look into that black box.

He hurried forward and pushed through the red brocaded curtains that had been hung across the far entrance. When the thick cloth brushed across his face, he shuddered.

The next room was strewn with half-dressed human figures, broken mannequins and models, bald-headed apparitions of pseudo-flesh, dummies with missing arms and legs, all stacked and piled together, many costumed in elaborate garb that must once have been colourful but now seemed faded, fragile, and ancient.

Tom moved between the figures, then walked up a ramp to a door clearly marked "EXIT."

It was a relief to see something as ordinary as that sign.

He shoved at barred doors that reminded him of a theatre exit; they parted and he found himself in a kind of shed. A dim ceiling bulb threw some faint light around the place. An old baby carriage, a pile of hubcaps, a canoe with a broken frame, and a few unidentifiable metal parts — all these had been shoved into the narrow space between two ancient black limousines.

There was also a late model girl's bicycle, with a straw hat dangling pink ribbons hung over the handlebars.

Tom wondered where he had come to, but sensed that he was finally out of the funhouse labyrinth. To get away from this place forever, all he had to do was scramble over this junk and find the street.

He started to exit, but before he could get anywhere the shed doors opened and a girl walked in.

She moved forward between the limousines, stopped in her tracks, and stood staring at him.

Tom stared back at her. He could not open his mouth. She was about his age, tall and slender with a pale oval face, curly dark hair, and delicate hands that she raised in surprise when she saw him. Dressed in a simple white T-shirt and jean shorts, she looked elegant, and somehow free. Tom felt joy in just looking at her.

She said nothing and uttered no murmur of surprise. She only looked at him intently with her dark blue eyes.

Tom took a deep breath and wrestled with conflicting thoughts. This was the most beautiful girl he had met in his short life. At the same time, she reminded him of someone.

"Who ... who are you?" he murmured. "I was down there" — he pointed behind him — "and the thing just started up. I went right through the tunnel. I'm looking for Mercury House."

Her eyes conveyed that she understood him, but she said nothing. Instead, she pointed to her lips and shook her head.

Tom stared at her, but his joy had turned into dismay, for it was clear that the girl couldn't speak.

Chapter Thirteen

Unknown Friends

Tom climbed up on one of the limousines, walked gingerly across the roof, slid down the windshield, then shoved himself feet-first across the dusty hood.

As he dropped down beside her, the girl smiled, took his hand, and pointed quickly at the doorway.

They stepped out of the shed together and she led the way along a narrow path enclosed by a half-fallen fence and lit by a few dim yellow bulbs.

He had a thousand questions for her, but he couldn't say a single word. His experience in the tunnel, their strange meeting, the night and this walk, the sense of her presence beside him, her affliction — these things made him silent.

He was certain, however, that he had found the girl who had sent him the ring, and it made him glad. She sailed along just in front of him, and her every step seemed to make his own body lighter. He felt that he was on the verge of some great discovery, that some rare magic had descended into his world at last.

They came 'round another shedlike building and he saw the house, a great black hulk of a place, with a single light burning on a big shabby rear porch. The amusement park stretched away behind them. He knew he must have entered the old tunnel from Harbour Street and circled on the underground track to the shed where he'd come out. But who had turned on the machinery? A puzzle! Everyone in West Hope knew that the old park was just a ruin.

They climbed up on the porch and she stopped for a minute, turned to him, reached out, took his hand, and turned it up so that the ring was clearly visible. Then she smiled at him and her dark eyes glinted with yellow fire. Her touch was gentle but tremendous. It occurred to him that she might be smiling at the idea of a dream being realized, for that was his experience at that moment — a moment so perfect he hoped it might never end.

Inside the house it was cool and dark: the kitchen they entered a moment later had ancient fittings, old linoleum, a battered tin sink, and a slow-dripping tap. The walls, where they were not covered with pictures and much-out-dated calendars, seemed waxen with grease and grime. The girl motioned him to a place at a big table, a noble relic with lion's feet, overhung by a ceiling light with a green glass shade.

She fetched a large pad from a bulletin board and wrote on it. She handed it to him and then pointed at herself.

Miranda Daniel, it said.

He looked at her in astonishment. She smiled, but he felt the anger rising in him. Of course he had seen her! He had caught a glimpse of her in Tarn's film — this was Paul Daniel's daughter, a victim of her own father's betrayals. It was Paul Daniel's fault that she had lost the ability to speak.

Tom started to say something, but stopped as she wrote again on the pad.

He read: *I sent the ring*, looked at her, and managed a smile. She seemed to sense his conflicting feelings, so she took the pen and added, *I saw you at the Blanchard High essay contest in first year. I know exactly what you wrote. I still keep it.* Ad astra per aspera — *when I found that saying I thought of you. That was what your essay said to me.*

He stared at her. Someone had noticed him. She'd been thinking of him all these years!

Once again she wrote and he read: *I saw you last year at Damato's. You didn't even notice me!*

He couldn't believe this and shook his head with vigour. And just at that moment, he remembered. She had come in at lunchtime one day and he wanted to get over to her table to talk to her, but he was hesitant, and the place was so busy that Willy had sent him out for extra bread. When he got back — much later — she'd left, and he'd never even noticed that she couldn't talk!

Now he put his hands together and bowed his head as if asking her pardon. She laughed and wrote on the pad: *My father has been talking to you.*

Tom shrugged his shoulders and waited for more. Now it would come, he thought, what a hard life he'd had, how we all had to be forgiving! Well, he wouldn't accept any of that, not even for her sake.

My father needs your help. Fabricon hurt him. They caused this.

Miranda touched her mouth with her fingers.

Tom shook his head in consternation. "But Tarn told us it was all your dad's fault. They seemed to have proof of everything."

She shook her head, almost with violence, seized the pad, and wrote hastily.

Lies! They framed him. He needs your help. Come!

Before he could react she was out of her chair and beckoning him through the doorway and into an inner room.

He followed her as she climbed a wide staircase whose carpeting had grown shabby, perhaps because it was nearly as old as the ornately carved banister. He caught glimpses of heavy drapes, old oil paintings with little lights set on top, oriental rugs in profusion, and a huge stained glass window illuminated from behind and apparently depicting St. George defeating the dragon.

She led him down a second-floor corridor and stopped before an oak-panelled door. She turned to Tom with a cautioning look, then knocked.

A voice growled from inside: "So bring the hero in!"

Miranda pushed the door open and entered. Tom followed. An old man in a wheelchair rolled toward them.

"It's about time!" the man said. "I hope you enjoyed my labyrinth! But where's your grandfather? We thought Sandalls might be hanging around somewhere out there. Well, at least we got one of you. My name's Zak Daniel. Pardon me if I don't shake hands."

He turned up his elbows — spreading out his arms as if he were conducting — and Tom saw that his fingers had been disfigured by some disease.

The man was dressed in a white collared shirt and wore an old-fashioned plaid bow tie. He was small and slender and obviously full of fire. Every time he spoke his long, curly white hair shook like a mane. Otherwise, he looked like a rich, retired jockey.

"Miranda and I were just getting acquainted," Tom said. Zak Daniel's smile was kindly.

"Getting acquainted! I should hope so. Ever since we heard you were at odds with Fabricon we've been trying to corral you. Of course Miranda knew your talents way back when, right honey?"

Miranda blushed and nodded and the old man continued.

"I presume my son sent you. We saw you out there on Harbour Street just dawdling around. Couldn't figure out why. When you went into the old tunnel I told Miranda to set the machinery going. We figured you'd enjoy the ride, though she seemed a bit hesitant to put you in motion! I knew the machinery was fine. I keep it that way. Tried it out myself only last year. They don't make rides like that any more. Can't wait until we can open the place up again!"

Miranda waved her arms as if to slow him down. She looked pleadingly at Tom and then at her grandfather.

"I understand, honey. You want me to explain things properly to this young fella. Fine. Well, why don't you go get him a cold drink or something and I'll start to fill him in?"

He waved Tom into a chair as Miranda slipped out of the room.

The old man rolled his wheelchair into the open doorway, peered down the hall, then returned slowly to his place by the bed.

"It's not permanent, you know," he whispered to Tom. "Not like this." He held up his twisted hands. "I guess her father didn't tell you. She was one of the first victims of Fabricon. She's making progress every day and can say a few sentences now and then. But it's hard for her and she sure needs encouragement. I hope you can help her."

Tom nodded eagerly. How he wanted to help her!

"Paul Daniel didn't send me here," he explained. "I came because I got a ring."

The old man whistled. "So Miranda sent it, did she? One of Marvin Cormer's old Mercury Man specials! Oh, I remember the magic of those rings! Kids loved them. But there aren't many left — you must be the first to get one in fifty years! I'll show you more wonders in a minute, though."

He motored his chair closer to where Tom sat and fixed him with his sharp glance.

"First, let me fill you in — you seem a little doubtful about us. Anyway, you have a right to know what you're getting into." Zak Daniel braced himself and closed his eyes for a second, as if he were fetching up difficult memories.

"About ten years ago my son went to work for the company that eventually became Fabricon. Tarn didn't work there then, nor that smarmy front man, Binkley, either. Paul was a psychologist with the firm — they were starting to hire them then. Needed 'em for both external and internal reasons. Everything was fine until Tarn and Binkley came on board. Pretty soon my son found he wasn't being included in decisions that were part of his expertise. Hell, I don't understand that stuff, but as he put it to me, they were just quietly shutting him out. To compensate for that they promoted him.

"Time passed. Then a couple of years ago they began to recruit kids — all very community-minded, or so it seemed. They've always claimed they were just showing the kids films and updating them on the latest hardware and software, but Paul began to suspect otherwise. He suspected that they were using them as guinea pigs. That was when things got a bit complicated."

Zak Daniel began to explain about later developments at Fabricon, things his son had noticed but couldn't quite make sense of, things he couldn't get straight answers about. As the old man spoke, moving his hands nervously over the buttons on his chair, Tom was aware that he was controlling his anger, trying to tell everything in sequence and as coolly as possible, and not quite succeeding.

"In the end Paul decided that Tarn and Binkley didn't want him there at all. He couldn't figure out why they didn't fire him until one day they made him a proposition. They wanted to buy us out and take over the park here — part of their plans for expansion. They were trying to ingratiate themselves with Paul, but when they found out that I wouldn't sell, they started to play rough."

Zak Daniel sniffed and cleared his throat.

"They framed my son — accused him of embezzling funds and stealing company secrets. There was a trial and he was convicted. But their case wasn't airtight — no wonder! — and he got a suspended sentence. He had to sit in jail for six months.

"They miscalculated when they went after my son. Yes sir! He had been all the while getting the goods on those swine. Not stealing secrets but tapping into their plan to create a —" Zak Daniel stopped in mid-sentence, shook his head, and continued. "Well, it's pretty horrible. But maybe Paul should explain it. I don't know how their technology works; I only know that it's immoral and won't do any good in this world. I'm all for blowing the whistle on them. It would be sweet revenge at that!"

Tom looked at the old man. What monstrous thing was Tarn planning? All his suspicions had been right!

He got up and paced across the room. "But why didn't your son just go after them? Why didn't he bring this up at his trial? He could have threatened to expose them. They would have caved in if they'd known he had their secret."

Zak Daniel shook his head. His mouth twisted into a bitter smile. "No way. He had to have evidence. They struck first, you see, and destroyed his credibility. He was thrown in jail. Then our brave Miranda went to work for them. She tried to infiltrate Fabricon, using her grandmother Cormer's first married name. She hoped to get the evidence to free her father, but Fabricon's program got her. They put her in the Pavlov Room and you see the results. When Paul got out of jail and learned what had happened, he wanted to blow up the place, but I persuaded him to wait. Then you came along."

For a few minutes, Tom sat in silence. He had been led to Miranda by his longing for an adventure, for a porthole into a new reality. Now he had found a new realty, but it wasn't so wonderful. It was terrifying. But at least it gave him an opportunity. Miranda had cared for him even before he contacted her. They were destined for each other, it seemed. He felt a thrill of joy.

Now she appeared at the door with a tray. She smiled at him as she set out a pitcher of juice and three glasses. Zak Daniel seemed to have buried himself for a moment in evil memories.

Tom went over and patted the old man's twisted hands. Miranda looked agitated. She paced the room, pointing to her lips and attempting to speak. She got out a few syllables, a word. "Help," she said. Then she sat down and scribbled something in her notebook.

My father has been watching Fabricon. He needs to get in there. You did it. You got in. You've got to help him. He knows where to find the evidence.

Tom read this with mounting excitement, then, hesitating for a moment, handed the notebook to her grandfather, who glanced at it quickly and said, "That's exactly it. As you see, I can't help much, and Paul wouldn't risk Miranda. But you and your grandfather — now that's a different story. If you were willing to help him ..."

Tom remembered Tarn's crazy speech at Damato's. With mounting anger he recalled how the scientist had tried to paint Paul Daniel as a thief and to turn Tom against him. Conditioning. That's what his grandfather had rightly called it, but it was worse than that. Tarn was using everyone, playing on their weaknesses, and for one reason only: *to create something monstrous.*

Miranda poured more juice for her grandfather. Tom watched her, aware now of what she must have suffered, of the traumas that had deprived her temporarily of her speech. At that moment Tom could have killed Tarn on the spot.

"I'd be happy to help your son, Mr. Daniel. I'll do anything I can to expose Tarn and his company."

Miranda crossed the room, and before Tom knew what was happening, she kissed him on the cheek.

He blushed, and the old man in the wheelchair nodded his head in satisfaction and told him, "I'd kiss you, too, except you wouldn't like it as much. ... Now there's something I have to show you. I'm glad you sent Tom the ring, Miranda."

Zak Daniel winked at Tom as his granddaughter turned shyly away. The boy was standing in a quiet kind of ecstasy, the scent of Miranda's hair lingering on his cheek and forehead.

"You know, Tom, it may not look like much, but this place has great potential. When I married Mary Cormer after poor Marvin's death we made some awesome plans. We were going to have an entertainment empire, Cormer Incorporated. After we developed Mercury Man Comics we were going to refurbish this place. We had some ideas for new rides and things — a few of them later developed by Disney. We were going to be rich, and Marvin's name was going to be a household word all over America. ... Unfortunately, none of it ever happened."

Tom waited for an explanation, but Zak Daniel simply shook his head. His glance was turned downward; he stared at his twisted hands as if they had somehow betrayed him. At that moment the past seemed like a weight on the old man, pressing hard on his shoulders, reminding him of missed opportunities, failed prospects.

Miranda wrote something on the pad and shoved it under her grandfather's eyes. He stared at it for a moment, then looked up and nodded.

"By golly, you're right! It's not too late yet! What would I do without you, Miranda?" His machine whirred into motion. "C'mon, Tom, I've got something to show you."

He cruised around his enormous bed, past a great oak dresser and an ancient standing lamp, and stopped at a door marked with a small brass plaque. Stepping closer, Tom saw that the plaque read: "MERCURY HOUSE ENTERPRISES."

Miranda came over, took Tom's hand, and squeezed it. Her dark eyes were full of excitement, and Tom was sure he was about to be shown something special.

When Zak Daniel swung the door back and switched on the light, Tom saw that they were in a kind of gallery, a high-ceilinged room spacious enough to hold a couch and tables, as well as an enormous array of bulky cabinets and piles of storage boxes. A giant TV was built into one wall, and along the other wall were hung large full-colour posters. Amazed, Tom recognized at once the familiar figure of Mercury Man, in full tilt against Nazis and gangsters, his powerful fists battling for peace and justice against a host of slouching, grinning enemies.

"There he is." Zak Daniel pointed proudly at the illustrations. "We had these posters made after Marvin's death. And in those cabinets we have all of Marvin's drawings — he had a host of ideas for new creations. Most of the original issues of the comic are there, too. I've never let them out of my sight. I have all kinds of memorabilia here. Some good old TVs, windup 78 speed players, old cameras, you name it. In some of the space back there we have stuff from the park, too. I've kept just about everything. Got a couple of fellows who keep the machinery running for me. They like to ride on it. They're sworn to secrecy, but I'm gonna cut them in when we get started again. Now, look at those photographs! Here's Marvin with Mary, and later with me."

He pointed to a display beside several piles of LP records. A kindly looking man in glasses, wearing the uniform of the American army, stood beside a slender dark-haired woman in a small print dress. "Lovely girl, Mary. Took great care of me after I got sick, but never coddled me. I miss her in every way. Thank God she died before Paul's troubles!"

Tom looked around; he felt a past world opening up to him, a world where things were simpler, more innocent. Or so it seemed.

"One more surprise," Zak announced. "The *pièce de résistance*, you might say. Something Mary made, just for the fun of it. I keep it in the next room right through there. Let's have a look at it!"

Zak steered his chair between the artifacts and pictures, obviously heading for a broad wooden doorway at the far end of the passage. Tom and Miranda followed slowly. The old man hadn't quite reached his goal, however, when the door was flung wide open. Brakes screeching, the wheelchair stopped in its tracks. Zak cried out. Miranda held tight to Tom's hand.

A figure stood in the doorway, a tall man, lithe and muscular and somewhat larger than life. He was dressed in a red jersey — the chest emblazoned with a staff and twining snakes. A bright red hood covered his face, but his eyes, gazing at them through narrow slits, seemed to pierce them where they stood. As he stepped forward, the man's blue cape swirled behind him, and blue tights showed the powerful build of his legs, while his feet appeared to be shod in red slippers winged with gold.

It was as if the comics, the posters — and some of Tom's private dreams — had suddenly come to life.

"Mercury Man!" he cried out.

His exclamation was almost drowned out, however, by Zak Daniel's prolonged and joyful snort, a noise that seemed to express both amazement and appreciation together.

"Well, I'll be darned!" the old man bellowed. "I'll be darned three times over! That is one hell of an idea!"

Chapter Fourteen

Trophies and Connections

Zak Daniel's laughter filled the room. Miranda ran up to the costumed figure and threw her arms around him. Tom stood in astonishment as Jack Sandalls stepped through the doorway behind Mercury Man, greeted Tom with a smile, and proceeded to introduce himself to the man in the wheelchair.

"Always wanted to meet you, Mr. Daniel," he said. "Heard you were some kind of eccentric and thought I'd probably like you."

"I've heard the same about you, Captain. You're a collector, I gather. What do you think of this?"

He waved his arm, indicating the displays on every side. Jack looked around and nodded in appreciation. "Yeah, I've been seeing some pretty amazing things. I didn't realize Marvin Cormer had left so much behind."

"You haven't seen anything yet," Zak Daniel told him.

Mercury Man pulled his hood down to reveal the face of Paul Daniel.

"Captain Sandalls has something big for us, Zak," he told his father. "It seems the police are having second thoughts about Fabricon. Someone may be leaking stuff to them. A special squad's been watching the company and trying to gather evidence against Tarn. They may have drawn a blank so far, but they have their suspicions."

"Wow!" Zak Daniel wheeled himself closer to his son's caped figure.

"I'd just finished my library research and my little survey of my police contacts when your son found me," Jack added. "I was happy to give him the good news. I couldn't figure where you'd got to, Tom, but I'm glad you're here."

"A ring brought him," Zak explained, and winked at his granddaughter, "and I'm very glad of it! But the costume! It's an inspiration. It may be the answer! How did you think of it?"

Paul Daniel shook his head and swung his blue cloak over one shoulder. "Don't know what you're talking about, Father — although I'm beginning to guess. I was just trying on the old outfit for Captain Sandalls when you appeared. We were going to surprise you with it."

Zak's slender body seemed to gyrate in the wheelchair. "Surprise is right! And you don't see it? It's our ticket into Fabricon! Mary, thank you! My wife Mary made it, you know. The Tom Strong outfit, too. We can use them both — that is, if Captain Sandalls — if Jack here — will allow Tom to help us. You do want to be part of this, Tom?"

Tom stepped forward. "You bet I do," he said.

"What are you talking about?" Jack asked. "What do these old costumes have to do with it? They're wonderful, of course, and I can see Mary Cormer made them with loving care, but what good are they to us? They won't scare anybody at Fabricon."

"It's not a question of *scare*," Zak Daniel explained. "It's a question of throwing dust in their eyes — of gaining time and opportunity. Now that we know that the police are wise to the Fabricon bunch we can take a risk to expose that gang. I've got an idea!"

"Let's hear it, then," Paul Daniel said. "But in your bedroom and after I get this outfit off. It's getting warm in here."

"All right. But show Tom the things in the back storeroom — the Tom Strong outfit especially. See if it fits him. We've got some planning to do before the night's over. I'll show Captain Sandalls some of our other mementos. Then we'll talk!"

Paul Daniel led Tom through the door and into the inner room. Miranda followed, smiling.

Tom looked around in amazement. If anything, this room was larger than the first one, and here too the walls were covered with posters and photographs; there were glass cases containing bits of memorabilia and boxes stacked all the way to the far end, where another broad stairwell led downward.

Yet despite its colourful exhibits, the room smelled musty and private. It seemed to Tom to be saturated with the past and with locked-up dreams.

Miranda broke in on this reflection. She pointed to a figure in the far corner, a caped model that seemed about to leap over an old pinball machine and come at them. From his grandfather's comics, Tom recognized it as a replica of Mercury Man's sidekick, Tom Strong, striking in black tights, a small black mask that gave him a somewhat roguish look, and a yellow cloak. Shiny yellow boots and a white jersey emblazoned with a red serpent that resembled a stylized bolt of lightning completed the outfit. Beside this apparition stood a somewhat larger twin, a blank-faced mannequin, bald and ridiculous, from which the Mercury Man costume had clearly just been removed.

"Miranda, leave me with Tom for a moment, will you?" Paul Daniel put his arm around his daughter. She looked happy, and Tom guessed that she was pleased to see him with her father at last.

"We'll join you after he tries on the costume," Paul Daniel went on. He had started to strip off his own colourful outfit. "Right now we have to talk."

Miranda slipped away and Tom began to peel off his clothes. Paul carefully removed the Tom Strong outfit from the mannequin and handed it to him, piece by piece. When he was fully dressed, Tom put on the black mask, peered at himself in the mirror, laughed, and flexed his muscles comically.

"Don't worry — it suits you fine," Paul Daniel said. "You're a well set-up kid. But there are a couple of things I want you to consider before you do anything rash."

They sat together on a long bench and Paul Daniel addressed Tom in his calm, slow manner.

"I'm glad Miranda got in touch with you. You can imagine what it's been like to have her shut up here so much — just because the world out there believes that I'm a criminal. A while ago Dad switched her to a private school, and we've had home lessons for her, too, but she hasn't been happy at all. She's a wonderful girl and she's going to be all right. I can see you like her and I'm glad."

Tom took a deep breath and waited. After a brief silence, Paul Daniel continued. "When I found out you had something on Fabricon and Tarn I was ecstatic. I watched, I waited — I had to be careful, because I thought they might con you."

"They almost did," Tom told him. "I'm sorry."

Paul Daniel slapped him on the shoulder. "I know. Your grandfather told me. But now you know the truth. Your grandfather's news is incredible. With that information we can go after them, and we even have some hope of sympathy from the police — so long as we don't screw things up."

Tom nodded. Suddenly the dreary city seemed exciting, while this storeroom, with its fantastic pictures and its models, was no longer a cabinet of toys: it was the centre of action, the centre of reality.

"Inside Fabricon there are computer files that will blow their whole conspiracy. They haven't been able to clean them up because they themselves need the information. I know exactly where those files are and I intend to go after them."

"Mr. Daniel — Zak — seems to have a plan."

"Yeah, and I'm pretty sure I know what it involves. It probably involves you and your grandfather, for a starter."

"We want to be part of it."

"That's fine, but there's one other person involved. You know who I mean?"

Tom shook his head. "Miranda?" he guessed.

"I mean your mother. I saw her a couple of times while I was watching your apartment. She seems like a fine, decent woman. We have to make sure that she knows what's happening."

Tom remembered. Tomorrow was the day of the company party. Chuck Reichert would be pitching for the supermarket softball team. She wanted Tom to be there, to be with her and with Reichert, whom she would be marrying some day.

All of a sudden Tom felt miserable again.

"Don't worry!" Paul Daniel reassured him. "I think I can make her understand. But if she has the least objection to whatever lunacy my dad's got planned, then you're gonna have to pull out of it. Agreed?"

Tom nodded his head slowly. "Agreed."

In the middle of pulling on a T-shirt, Paul Daniel stopped, seemed about to speak, then hesitated.

"What is it?"

"One more thing. You know something about what Fabricon's doing, and eventually you'll learn more. I don't believe in breaking the law, but if you think about what they're up to, the situation changes. They really think that human beings are ultimately just flesh machines, that they can play with us and reprogram us once they know enough about our biological makeup. Fabricon is bad enough, but when I think who they might sell their secrets to it scares the hell out of me."

"But what exactly are they trying to do?"

"We'll talk about that later. Let's put it this way: they have a program that I find pretty terrifying."

"You really think their program can work?"

Paul Daniel shook his head. "I believe it can, although how far they can go with it, I don't know. Nobody does. Not yet. The point is, Tom, I hate what they stand for. They have a contempt for human beings. It's never occurred to them that there's an *X* factor in everyone, something they can't touch, something that has to do with the old-fashioned word *soul*."

"Soul?"

"Call it a kind of metaprogramming, or higher functioning, if you like. This is something you have to remember, Tom — that freedom is a very precious thing, and it depends on our ability to be ourselves, to be human in the best way we can. As far as I can see, that's where *soul* comes in."

Paul Daniel stood up. He didn't look at Tom, but without another word he turned and walked out of the room.

Tom followed him through the corridor, past the photographs and displays, and back toward Zak Daniel's bedroom. From that direction, just then, roars of laughter sounded. His grandfather and Zak Daniel were obviously hitting it off very well.

He found them in close conversation. Zak was already tucked in bed; Jack sprawled in a chair beside him. A bottle of whiskey sat on the night table between them.

"Come and have a drink, Paul," Zak said. "But only a small one. We want your head clear so that you can size up this plan of mine!"

The three men laughed. "We'll get sandwiches in a minute," Zak went on. "I'm almost tempted to suggest a restaurant ... haven't been out to a restaurant in five years or more. But no, we don't dare go out — we can't risk being seen together. We'll make our plans right here, and then we can go our separate ways — until D-Day, anyway."

Miranda beckoned to Tom and he followed her slowly down the stairs. He watched her carefully as she descended in front of him. It was funny; he felt himself constantly staring at her, almost as if he was trying to memorize what she looked like. Yet every time he gazed at her (her eyes, her hair, her bare knees) he felt a pleasant shock of surprise, as if he were seeing something new and wonderful.

In the kitchen she pulled a manila folder from a pile of papers on the counter. Inside was a newspaper clipping, and when he read it Tom was astounded to find that it recorded his first-year high essay triumph. "YOUTH ADVISES 'REACH FOR THE STARS,'" the caption read, and went on to describe how Tom had beaten out every student in the city with his eloquent prose. Just a year ago he had reread the essay and had found it ridiculously simple-minded. He would have thrown away his copy of the frayed clipping, and the essay too, except that he knew his mother would have been horrified.

Now, with Miranda smiling at him, he was very glad to have been the author of the piece. That she had enjoyed it and kept it was almost a miracle.

Even that miracle became as nothing, however, when — without any preamble — she crossed the room to where Tom stood, took his ringed hand in hers, and squeezed it gently. He smiled — awkwardly, he felt, for she was very close — and looked into her deep blue eyes.

This is perfect — he felt it with his mind and body together. But there was more, for, holding his fingers in a tight grasp, she said in a low, small, but very distinctive voice the single word: "Welcome."

CHAPTER FIFTEEN

The Computer from Hell

Tom's mother paced up and down the room. The apartment seemed to shrink around her.

"It's not possible!" she said, for the third or fourth time. "It's just not possible."

Jack squirmed on the couch and once again tried to explain. "I've talked to the police," he said. "They're more or less on our side, Karen. Otherwise we wouldn't think of going in."

"Rubbish! You'd do it no matter what they said. And when you talk about the police, I know what you mean: you mean a few old boozing cronies who think the same way you do. And what happens if everything goes wrong? I don't want my son with a criminal record, thank you!"

"Mom!" Tom started to object, but thought better of it. His grandfather had given him a look. Paul Daniel, who had said nothing so far, sat on a chair by the kitchen door. To Tom's amazement, his usual grim expression had softened; he seemed to be controlling himself, enjoying the situation, barely suppressing a smile.

Tom hoped Paul wouldn't laugh at his mother. All hell would break loose if he did. He'd never seen her so angry or so frustrated. At any moment, he thought, she might burst into tears.

"I just don't believe that you couldn't trust me," she continued. "That you got into all this without letting me know. God — talk about chauvinism! A bunch of silly boys who have to protect me from reality. Who think it's a game to break into a respectable business, just because they have a few wild suspicions about what's going on inside."

"Mrs. Blake —" Paul stood up. He crossed the room, intercepted her, and held her gently by the arm. He was serious now.

"I understand how you feel, Karen. But a lot of things are at stake here. I'm thinking of my family, too. You understand that I have to clear my name. And, believe me, our suspicions are based on fact."

"What facts? You haven't told me anything yet."

Paul Daniel gently steered her toward the sofa. To Tom's amazement his mother let him do this. She settled down, took a deep breath, and gave Paul Daniel a close, searching look. It was as if she were seeing him for the first time.

"I don't know ... I just don't know," she murmured. "You can't expect me to approve of this. Surely there's a better way."

"There's no other way, Karen," Paul said quietly. "I didn't want to have to tell you this — at least not until I had the proof to hand you. I haven't told anyone the whole story, not even my friends here." He waved in the direction of Tom and Jack. "We talked last night about how to break into Fabricon, I'll admit it, but even then I was being a bit cagey about what I knew. Frankly, I didn't want to disgust anyone."

"What we heard was bad enough already," Jack said. "And I've got a pretty strong stomach."

"Tell me and I'll make up my own mind," Karen said. "And I want Tom to know what he's getting into."

Paul nodded grimly. "Have you ever heard of the molecular computer?"

He looked at each of them in turn. Tom was baffled and the others looked equally blank.

"I thought not. You see, most computers are made of silicon strands, but the molecular computer is different. It's made of DNA."

Jack whistled softly. "You mean genetic stuff, the stuff of life? That sounds crazy!"

"It's not crazy at all. A California scientist discovered the possibility years ago. DNA is actually a digital entity — that means it can count. It fact, it can count like almost nothing on earth. Scientists agree on the fantastic capabilities of the molecular computer. It can calculate a hundred million billion things at once."

Tom shook his head. "Gosh, that would put today's computers to shame, wouldn't it?"

"Exactly. It would be the most incredible thinking machine in the history of the world."

"It sounds amazing," Karen said. "But why is it evil?"

"Like most scientific discoveries, it's not evil at all," Paul explained. "Whether it's evil or not depends on how responsibly you use it, and what you have to do to create it."

Tom leaned forward, listening closely as Paul continued in his quiet monotone. "DNA chips can be implanted in the human body. They can serve good purposes, such as monitoring illness, but they can also be used to manipulate people. Tarn has not only taken advantage of this, but he's gone much further. I'm sure he talked a lot of grandiose nonsense to you two in the restaurant — he's good at that. But let me tell you what I discovered ..."

Paul Daniel got up and began to pace the room. "When Tarn came to Fabricon, he decided to jump ahead of the world's scientists to create a very special super DNA computer. So instead of using just any DNA material, he decided to base his computer on human brain tissue."

Tom shuddered and found himself rubbing his hand across his forehead, as if his grey cells were already under threat.

"That sounds horrible," Karen said.

"It is horrible. Tarn's idea is that with human brain tissue he can create a DNA computer that will itself be a kind of ultra programming machine, one that will be able to manipulate us absolutely because it would be constructed of living human material, *of thinking matter*. Such a machine — or genetic super-being, which is what it would really be — might well find ways to control whole populations, to reshape the whole planet."

"What's the poor world coming to?" moaned Jack. "Destruction, I greatly fear, if Tarn has his way."

"It could well be. He's worked out a three-stage plan. Stage one, recruit bright young people and condition them so that they would be docile enough to be used as guinea pigs. Stage two, take them in a hypnotized state to the Pavlov Room and scan and map their brains for a later operation. Stage three, take actual genetic brain material from them and recombine the DNA in order to produce the world's most powerful DNA computer. It's significant that Tarn was going to call that room Pavlov, after the famous scientist. Pavlov experimented on and controlled rats or dogs, but this computer could be used to control not only the machinery of society, but *our very thought processes themselves.* Once this monster gets built, there's no telling what will happen to human beings on this earth."

"God Almighty, that Tarn's some kind of Dr. Frankenstein," Jack said. "And he's out to build the computer from hell."

"You're right, but he's worse than Frankenstein. This isn't an experiment with dead matter. This involves real living people. And some of them have already been hurt by it."

Tom swallowed hard. He thought of what Zak Daniel had told him about Miranda. He understood now why Paul had wanted to bomb the company. But evil shouldn't be answered with evil, he was sure of that.

"There's your horror," Paul said. "The man will stop at nothing. But I know where the evidence is and I have to go and get it. I won't succeed on my own, but if you don't want Tom to go in there with me, Karen, I'll go anyway. I can understand your feelings as a mother, believe me I can. But maybe you can understand my feelings as a father. My daughter infiltrated the program to try to vindicate me. The conditioning affected her negatively; she lost her speech and it's taken her many months to regain any of it. Thanks to Tom here, she's getting better by the hour, but it's been a sad time for all of us."

Karen bowed her head. Everyone was silent. Then she said, "But can you beat them? If you get the evidence, won't they just buy their way out of it? Is it a good idea to break the law?"

"I've waited too long already," Paul said. "You know that when Tom and his friends went for jobs in the spring they got turned away by Fabricon. Now it's only mid-summer and all the kids are being welcomed with open arms. It's clear that the experiments began a while ago, then stopped while Tarn evaluated the results. Now they're beginning again and he needs more people, more kids, more victims. *They're heading into the final phase.* If Tom hadn't scouted out their premises, if we hadn't connected, no one would be challenging them. No, Karen, nothing can stop me from going in. They may arrest me but at least I'll have tried."

A silence fell over the room. Finally, Paul stood up and said, "This isn't getting us anywhere. Maybe I should get out of here and just let you three work it out.

I'm going to wait in my truck downstairs. It was nice to meet you, Karen."

Tom's mother looked at him; she seemed to be meditating on something. They stood in the centre of the room and shook hands. "It was nice to meet you, Paul," she murmured. "And believe me, I wish you nothing but the best."

But as soon as Paul Daniel had disappeared, she started in again.

"Jack, you're an idiot!" she told him. "And you" — she turned a searching glance on Tom — "of course it would have been too much for you to talk to me, to your own mother. I always said I wanted to hear about what was going on in your life. But no, you had to shut me out. Now you see the result."

"I'm sorry, Karen," Jack said. "It's my fault that it worked out this way. We didn't even know half these things, Tom and I ... but I'm committed to help Paul, you understand."

"I've *got* to help him, Mom," Tom told her.

"That's fine for both of you. But if this is going to happen — and I can see that you won't back down — I intend to be there. Besides, I want to meet this Miranda — and her grandfather, too, as a matter of fact."

Tom felt a thrill of joy when his mother said Miranda's name. It was as if some unspoken barrier had been broken. He looked at his grandfather; Jack Sandalls looked at Tom.

She was coming through for him. He wanted to hug her, to thank her.

There was a knock at the door. All three of them jumped.

"You see," his mother said, "we're acting like criminals already."

The door was flung open. Chuck Reichert stood there, outfitted for softball. He wore a baseball cap and a striped uniform that made him look like a convict. In his right hand he held a couple of bats; a catcher's mask and two mitts were slung on a cord over his right shoulder.

Reichert tipped up his sunglasses, looked at them expectantly, and said, "Play ball!"

"Oh my God!" Karen Blake shook her head and half-closed her eyes. Tom thought, *Maybe she's seeing Reichert for the first time.*

Chuck seemed to miss her expression. "How are you, buddy?" he asked, beaming at Tom. "Ready to hit a few good ones for the old A&P?"

"We're not going to the game," Tom said. "We have more important things to do."

"Tom!" his mother cautioned. He gulped and realized that he had nearly blown it.

"A family emergency's come up," Jack intervened. "It's a terrible shame, Chuck, but it looks like none of us can go."

Chuck Reichert gazed from one to the other. "What? Are you kidding? This has been planned for weeks. What's going on here?"

"It's my fault, Chuck," Karen Blake told him. "I'm a wicked woman. Did you see a man going out as you came in here?"

"A man? You mean the rangy guy with the black T-shirt and the heavy shades? Yeah, I saw him on the stairs. What about it?"

Tom's mother crossed the room, hesitated, then told him, "I'm sorry, Chuck. He's an old flame of mine. He's just turned up unexpectedly and he wants to buy us all lunch. He's into mountain climbing — that kind of thing — and now he's suddenly going to Nepal to teach. Leaving in a couple of hours, in fact. I can't very well refuse him, can I?"

"What? What are you talking about? You never told me about this guy! Why does he have to say goodbye to you? What about the damned game?"

Chuck Reichert looked at each of them in turn and shook his head. He shifted the gear on his shoulder, started to question them, but seemed suddenly at a loss for words.

"Don't worry, Chuck," Tom's grandfather said. "We'll get together later. We'll call you."

Karen Blake leaned over and kissed his cheek. "I sure hope the A&P wins," she said.

Reichert, his glance full of suspicion, muttered, "What in hell is going on here?"

"It's a family emergency," Jack reiterated. "Just like we said."

Still Reichert hesitated. He seemed to be waiting for Karen to say something, and when she remained tight-lipped, he hung his head like a guilty child.

"OK, OK … if you can come along later, you know where it is, Karen."

He turned and left quickly, not bothering to close the door. Tom clapped his hands in glee, but his mother said, "I felt rotten doing that to Chuck."

"A woman has to do what a woman has to do," Jack told her. Then he added, "But you can understand why we want to help Paul."

"Yes," she said, but didn't look at him.

"There are some things to get into the pickup," Tom said.

He felt excited. It seemed the last barrier had been crossed. The great adventure was beginning.

On the street, he struggled with two heavy boxes. Paul had parked half a block away and Tom could see his black truck waiting there. Paul himself was clearly visible, sitting placidly behind the wheel. But when Tom waved to him to pull closer, an odd thing happened — he ducked away suddenly and disappeared.

Tom blinked and looked around.

A car had pulled up beside him, a bright red sedan. The passenger windows rolled down, and Estella leaned out and smiled at him.

"Hi, Tom, like to go over to the casino?"

Tom was taken aback. She was heavily made up, dressed in a tight black blouse, and her eyes had a crazy glitter that he'd never seen there before.

Pete Halloran, in sports jacket, rollneck, and shiny slacks, sat next to her. He leaned over, giggled, and nodded at Tom's burdens.

"Hey, buddy, they got you working for a living?"

"I hope you've made things right with Dr. Tarn," Estella said. "We were going to give you a call."

"Yeah, we were afraid you'd be serving time by now," Pete added. He lifted a fat joint from the ashtray and gulped some smoke.

Tom, who had rested one hand briefly on the car door, was horrified to see that Estella had noticed his ring. He pulled his hand away quickly, but the girl giggled and said, "No, let me see it!"

"He's too shy!" Pete nudged her. "Doesn't want us to ask about his trinkets. Come on and smoke a joint with us, Tommy Buck. Then you can tell us about your secret life."

"It's a magic ring," Tom assured them. "I got it for a box top and a quarter."

They both laughed.

"That's a good one, Tom. We've got a magic ring, too — a smoke ring," Pete confided, and they laughed. "If you'd have gone with Fabricon in the first place, you wouldn't have to haul those parcels."

"I'm just doing something for my mom," Tom explained.

"Yeah? I guess she's the one who gave you the ring — is that it?"

Pete Halloran shook with laughter at his own wit. Estella put her hands to her eyes and giggled. Tom bent over and began to tug at the boxes.

"*Yo ho hee ho*!" Pete sang.

"Oh, shut up!" Tom muttered.

"See you later, Thomas," Pete called to him. To Tom's great relief the car window rolled up. He could see the two of them inside, talking and pointing at him. *My friends,* he thought bitterly, *my good friends.* Then the engine roared and the car disappeared down the dusty street.

As it roared past the black pickup, Paul reappeared behind the wheel. He had ducked out of sight in the cab, it seemed. Now he started the truck, and it rolled slowly in Tom's direction.

Tom stood there, frustrated and seething with anger. The kids had no idea what a threat was hanging over them. And to save them, he and Paul would have to take on Fabricon.

CHAPTER SIXTEEN

The Pavlov Room

Two hours later Tom stood in the tiny park opposite Fabricon. It was late afternoon but as hot as ever, and all the windows in the company tower seemed to be melting in the sunlight. Liquid gold, a fiery transformation, the terrifying moment before the irrevocable act. Tom looked down and touched his ring. He thought of Miranda, who was with her grandfather in Mercury House, a place very close to where he stood, yet just out of sight. He thought of his mother and grandfather, waiting around the corner in Paul Daniel's pickup.

Paul himself paced like a restless animal between the phone booth and the water fountain, juggling a few coins nervously in his right hand. The park was empty and Harbour Street seemed desolate on this lazy Sunday afternoon. Once again Paul glanced at his watch, but this time he stopped in his tracks, patted Tom gently on the shoulder, and announced firmly, "I guess it's now or never."

He slipped into the phone booth and quickly dialled a number. After a pause, and a few clearings of his throat, he said, "That you, Mac? This is Bob Allan, Special Events. Yeah, they've got me working today. I'm calling from downtown. About the kids' party. You haven't heard? For some city bigwigs and their brats. What'll they think of next, huh? Send up the costumed ones and the balloon man right away, OK? You can't miss them. I'll be over in a flash. Thanks!"

Tom marvelled at how easily Paul had changed his voice and tone. It was a masterpiece of impersonation.

"Let's move!" Paul said.

Together they ducked into the old stone public washroom, opened the bags they had hauled from the truck earlier, and began to change.

The lavatory was small and stank of bleach and urine. Its walls were scrawled over with filthy graffiti, yet the fixtures were shiny and ancient, almost elegant in aspect. When Tom peeled off his clothes, he dropped them on a white tiled floor that looked something like a grimy game board.

"Hope to God no one appears," Paul muttered. "We'll be arrested before we start."

Within minutes, however, they folded up their outer clothes and stuffed them into the bags. Out of the same bags had come the costumes, carefully pressed and stitched here and there by Miranda.

Within minutes Mercury Man and his sidekick Tom Strong stood together in front of the washroom mirror.

"Awesome," Tom pronounced, but his insides were

churning with anxious expectations. This was the craziest thing he had ever done — and the most dangerous.

"Let's go!"

Mercury Man dashed across the little park; Tom Strong followed. A bus was just pulling away from the Harbour Street stop and an elderly man, happening to look out the window, stared open-mouthed at the pair of them. They raced across Harbour Street. A few cars honked; drivers laughed and waved. Tom saw Paul Daniel's pickup pull into the Fabricon driveway.

"Right on time," Paul shouted.

He flung open the back door of the pickup and they tossed in the bags containing their clothes. At the same moment the passenger door opened and Jack Sandalls hopped out. He was carrying a string of brightly coloured balloons in one hand and a pink shopping bag covered with blue teddy bear decorations in the other.

"Well, if it isn't Mercury Man and his sidekick Tom Strong! Welcome to West Hope, guys!"

"Shut up and get moving," Paul growled at him. "Or we'll be entertaining in the State Pen."

Jack laughed and headed for the entrance. Tom waved to his mother, who had twisted around from her place in the driver's seat. She blew him a kiss and pulled the truck out of the driveway, spinning away down Harbour Street as Paul and Tom followed Jack through the Fabricon doors.

A lazy Sunday afternoon, and, as they had calculated, the front hall was nearly empty. On the left, near the company visual displays, a worker was mopping the floor. Mac the guard sat behind the desk reading a newspaper. He looked up as they approached, did a small double take, and laughed.

"The Bob Allan party bunch, I guess. Kids aren't here yet. You can go right up. Reception room on floor six. Take the elevator."

Tom breathed a sigh of relief.

"Here's a balloon for you," Jack said. The man chuckled, mumbled his thanks, and started to tie it to his chair.

They left him fumbling with the string and pushed into the inner corridor.

Mercury Man spoke in a fierce whisper.

"The elevator's for you, Jack. Leave the toys in the reception room and go out the back way. Remember, walk straight through the parking lot and look for the candy store. Karen will pick you up there. If all goes well, we'll meet you at the front entrance in twenty-five minutes. Good luck!"

"Same to you!"

The elevator came; it was empty. Jack stepped in. The doors closed, and the light went on.

Tom followed Mercury Man along the corridor, through a door marked "Private," and down a flight of stairs.

The storage rooms are in the basement, Paul had told them. *And I've still got my key.*

They pushed through the door at the bottom and came into another corridor. A man strolled out of a recessed area. He stopped beside a large poster of some

Swiss-like scenery, gaped at them, smiled, and started to say something.

Mercury Man slammed into him at top speed. The man crashed back through the doorway. The poster rattled and fell to the floor. Tom ran to help, but Mercury Man was up in a flash. He swung a hard right; the man toppled and lay still.

Tom said, "Wow!"

Now they saw that the room was full of tables, on which sat a few small monitors, some of them flashing with diagrams and data. Boxes of old floppy disks had been stacked in one corner. In the other was a cart carrying few old slide projectors. Printers were in evidence, and piles of documents tied with ribbon.

Together they dragged the dazed man to a narrow cupboard, rolled him in quickly, and locked the door.

Footsteps and voices in the corridor. Mercury Man waved a warning at Tom, tiptoed to the door, and pulled it shut.

"This stuff is nothing. I've got to get to the special files," he whispered. "I'll count three, you break out and go left. That should draw them off. Remember the diagram I showed you? I'll meet you at the main lounge in ten minutes."

Tom waited. The count took forever.

One ... two ... three!

He burst into the corridor and headed left. Two men stood in his way, one dressed in blue overalls, the other in a white lab jacket. They gave him startled looks, hesitated a second, then stepped aside as he dived past them.

He sprawled on the floor and was up again.

"Hey!"

"Who in hell's that?"

He heard their cries but wasn't stopping. The white walls flashed past. Paul had briefed him on the layout here. He cut to the left again and ran down a ramp and along a straight corridor. A man sat on a bench drinking coffee. As Tom ran past, the man did a double take, glanced suspiciously at his cup, and jumped up. He shouted something incomprehensible.

Tom ran on, sprinting by some metal stands, a row of bicycles, and a couple of drink machines. He was looking for the exit sign that led to the main underground parking. When he found it, he knew he could cut through the garage and come out near the main hall.

By now he was almost used to the Tom Strong uniform. It was terribly hot inside it and the mask cut off his vision, but the effect on those he met seemed stupendous.

Tom clenched his fists. *Would he really have the courage to attack someone, the way Mercury Man had done?* His yellow boots thumped on the hard floor, and his breath came short. He slowed down.

Suddenly, an alarm sounded all around him, a low-level but very nasty banshee scream, as if all the cars in the parking lot were being rifled at once. *Bad news.* He prayed that they hadn't caught Paul.

Still no exit sign. Had he made a wrong turn?

A man appeared from nowhere — he was four or five doors away — a big man, taking up most of the corridor, carrying something like a police nightstick.

He had a red face and massive shoulders. He didn't blink at Tom's uniform. Security cop, no question about it.

Tom hit the brakes and turned. No way to take on that guy. He wasn't Mercury Man yet.

More trouble. As he turned Tom saw the coffee drinker, now wide awake and pretty riled up, coming straight at him. Two or three others followed. A dog barked somewhere.

An old poem came into Tom's mind. "Cannon to the right of them! Cannon to the left of them! Into the valley of death, rode the six hundred."

"Not yet!" he cried. He flung open a door on his right and bounded up a short stairway, taking two steps at a time.

"We've got him now!" someone shouted.

Like hell you have, Tom thought, but they were right. At the top of the stairs there was only one way to go. Straight into a lab, a small room full of blank screens, a place that seemed to have no other exit.

Tom hesitated, pulled the door shut behind him, and locked it.

His heart pounded, all his senses were nervously alert, and the alarm's insane screeching drilled through his head like a spike. Yet he felt he might hold them at bay, do something, anything, to confound them — until he heard a voice outside in the corridor announcing, "We've got him! He's trapped in the Pavlov Room!"

Tom looked around, eyeing the blank walls, the multiple screens, with fearful apprehension. The Pavlov

Room! The very place he had wanted to avoid — Tarn's conditioning centre. He sprang for the door — no good. They would nab him at once.

He took a step back, his costume suddenly drenched in sweat. He was in for it now. Trapped in the heart of Fabricon, locked in the notorious Pavlov Room.

Did they have Paul, too? He didn't know.

Tom pounded on the door, kicked at it in sheer frustration, ran frantically from side to side.

No way out. The room was clean, almost antiseptic, and somehow more frightening for that. What were all the screens and monitors for? That white table? It was like an operating room where someone could take apart your brain.

There are three stages to the Pavlov Program, Paul had told them. *Mind control, the DNA probe, and the construction of the Mind Computer.*

And some of it was happening here, he thought.

All of a sudden the siren's clamour stopped. Maybe now he could think, get hold of himself. Tom closed his eyes, clenched his fists, and counted to ten. He looked around again. In two corners of the room, close to the ceiling, he saw cameras, small metal boxes rotating as he moved. Instruments that could track him, follow his panic dance. Who would be watching him?

It was impossible — they had him now. Desperately, he tried to think. *What would Tom Strong do?*

The first thing was to cut their advantages. He might neutralize the cameras.

Tom looked around, estimating the height of the lab table. If he could pile up a couple of boxes …

Eagerly, he set to work. He pushed the lab table into one corner, then fumbled in several drawers and cabinets, looking for an object with which he could strike at the cameras. In one drawer he turned up an old spike bar. It wasn't very heavy, but there seemed to be nothing else.

He piled up a couple of boxes and climbed until he could grasp the metal support that anchored the camera. Hanging on tight to keep his balance, he struck the thing blow after vicious blow, aiming as best he could for the lens. The spike bar bent and twisted, bits of metal rained down, and finally the camera itself hung askew and, as he hoped, useless.

Painstakingly, he pulled the table across the room and repeated the assault on the other camera. Just when it appeared he was achieving a similar result, all the lights in the room went out.

Tom gasped, clung to the twisted metal, and waited.

A woman's voice spoke admonishingly, almost in his ear. "This is private property. We have a good idea who you are and you can't get away. Climb down from your perch, sit calmly, and wait for your instructions. Dr. Tarn is going to speak to you in a minute."

Tom shook his head in frustration. There seemed to be nothing to do but to obey the instructions. He groped his way down in the darkness, bits of metal and glass clattering around him.

He groped for a chair, sat in the middle of the Pavlov Room, and waited.

A few minutes passed. Then a pleasant music started up, piped in around him, the monotonous caress of a bland repeated melody.

It was like being stuck in an elevator, washed over by muzak until you felt your brain deaden and your mind relax.

Tom sat there staring into the darkness until a screen full of images took shape in the air just before him.

Forms and colours floated before him, abstract patterns moving seductively against a limitless blue background. Tom looked away, looked back, yawned.

Other screens around him lighted up. Everything was gentle and muted — the music, the colours. Patterns that seemed related but not identical, swirls of lines, geometrical figures that appeared and dissolved — it was all very reassuring. He didn't think he should move. The woman's voice spoke to him again, gentle, persuasive — it touched his mind so lightly.

Do your arms feel very heavy?
Your legs too heavy to move?
Everything easy and relaxed,
And your eyelids heavy and heavier.
Breathe deeply and relax,
Relax, relax, relax …

His eyelids *did* feel heavy. His arms and legs were like lead. The tension was dissolving, and that was very good. He felt almost comfortable in his awkward chair. He pulled his mask off and threw it away. He closed his eyes.

Forget all your duties and the world out there.

We'll take care of everything.
Breathe deeply and relax.
Fabricon is your friend.
Fabricon is your friend.

The walls of the room seemed to fade away. Vistas spread out before him — pleasant landscapes, quiet flowing streams. He heard the gentle rustling of leaves in an endless forest. Everything calm and pleasant.

Relax and enjoy.
Fabricon is your friend.

Tom heard a voice echoing inside him, in a deep space inside his mind. In the middle of the sentence it was no longer a woman's voice but a man's, and the voice said:

I want you to lie down now and look up at the ceiling.
Lie on your back and look at the ceiling.

Tom had no hesitation in obeying. Not to obey would mean that all the tensions, all the threats would come back to him. He didn't want them. He wanted to be left alone, to relax, to be at peace.

He slid out of his chair and lay on his back on the floor.

The ceiling opened up. It was sky. Infinity. He seemed to be lifted.

Now comes the perfect moment.
Remember, Fabricon is your friend ...

The sky above him darkened. It was like a black well, something to drown in, oblivion. Tom felt himself falling upward, downward, into that pleasant soft sky.

Then he saw the stars, tiny points of light in the darkness. They began to circle, to move. He felt himself drawn to them, swallowed up …

A phrase came into his mind: *Ad astra per aspera.*

The ring! He sat up, peeled off the glove on his left hand, and touched the ring. He snapped open the top. Something flashed in the concealed mirror — a beam of light, a spark from his own soul? Paul Daniel had said it: *There's an X factor in everyone; something no Fabricon can touch.*

Tom thought of the beautiful Miranda, of Paul and his boldness and daring. He couldn't give up now.

The voice droned on in the background.

Relax. Listen carefully to what I say …

No!

Tom's whole being cried out against this subtle enemy. He had to fight, to save himself. He jumped to his feet, holding up one arm to shield his eyes from the dazzling light. His violent motion, his helter-skelter desperation, seemed to jolt his mind free, and after a few seconds he found he could think clearly again.

He looked around. *There must be a way to get out of here.*

Warily, he began to circle the room.

He moved relentlessly, flinging the screens aside, kicking at the monitors, pushing the tables. It didn't matter that, despite the ravaged cameras, Tarn might be watching him; he *hoped* he was watching him!

Tom kept circling, examining everything, wary as a fencer, then suddenly behind one of the largest screens he saw outlined on the antiseptic white of the wall the clear markings, the panelled shape, of a doorway.

A room? A secret way in and out? He clenched his sweating hands and looked around.

There seemed to be no tools, nothing to force the door. Perhaps there was a switch?

Sit down and relax.

Lie on the floor and relax.

Dr. Tarn will be with you soon.

Tom moved with frantic haste, pressing the panel everywhere with his fingers, kicking at the smooth walls. But it was no good; he couldn't find the lever.

He crashed down into a chair and in sheer frustration pounded his right fist on the smooth white table at his elbow ... *and the panel in front of him slid slowly open.*

He gasped and stood up. He was staring into an illuminated cave, an eerie locker full of twinkling lights. A cold breath of air touched his cheeks and forehead. The room made him think of a butcher's freezer.

He started to step in, stopped, then turned and pulled the chair into place, setting it so that it would block the panel should the wall slide shut behind him.

Having done this, he took a few steps forward, stopped, and gazed around.

Tom shivered; he felt as if his soul would freeze. But he hung on, forcing himself to look, taking in every detail, as Paul's warning sounded in his mind.

Phase two is the DNA Probe. They intend to take samples from all of you in order to construct their monster computer.

In the darkness he saw his friends — Jeff Parker, Estella Lopez, Bim Bavasi, Pete Halloran — as well as other kids he knew by sight or vaguely by name. There stood Estella with her dark eyes, Pete, and Bim with his mocking glance, surveying everything. For one horrible moment he thought he was looking at their frozen bodies.

But no! These were full-sized replicas, making a grisly show like a waxworks, lifelike in detail, and set there like displays in some ghoulish museum.

A steady bleating sounded, like the cry of a lost animal, underlined by the droning music of the air conditioners. Tom had noticed that on the wall behind each replica there was an illuminated diagram, one that showed what was obviously the structure of the human brain, and that each diagram was marked slightly differently.

There was a shaded portion here, an arrow there, and an eerie array of blinking coloured lights.

Although it was more complex and brilliantly illuminated, the display reminded him of the butcher's charts he had seen that showed the different cuts of meat on the animal.

Fabricon was clearly working on the next stage in the construction of its DNA computer. They were marking what they needed from each person's brain, where they would probe, what tissue or nerve they would tamper with.

They might be much further ahead than even Paul had imagined.

Tom took a step forward. Just beyond the replicas of his friends he saw another figure. It stood in lighted prominence on the darkest part of the wall.

It had its own niche, its own stance, its own peculiar hue of pink skin.

He stared at it in horror.

It was himself, his living semblance, yet it did not resemble anything living: it was a ghastly caricature, dead, cold, and terrible.

He stepped back, groaned, and buried his face in his hands.

They were preparing him for an experiment!

Tom turned and fled. Bumping into furniture and overturning chairs, he stumbled into the outer room. Groaning, he struggled to find a way out.

Just relax.

Dr. Tarn is on his way to see you now.

Tom ran to the main door and kicked at it. No good. He clenched his fists. He wouldn't be part of their experiment!

Suddenly he remembered something he had seen when he was smashing the cameras. A grid, a panel, close to the ceiling.

He climbed like a cat on the table and once again balanced precariously on the boxes. His fingers groped in the semi-darkness. Screens fluttered around him.

Just relax and keep looking into the deep sky.

We are about to take you on a little trip.

Patterns flickered above him but he didn't look. He groped along the smooth ceiling — and found the grid.

If only it screwed loose from his side!

It did. His fingers found first one knob, then another. Slowly, carefully, he unscrewed the plate.

Soon he had the whole plate loosened. Then he removed the screws, careful not to let the thing drop.

He turned it sideways and shoved it up into the opening. It clattered once and stayed. *Now*, he thought, *the tricky part*: he had to swing up, trusting to his ability to hang on.

Tom Strong could do it.

He swung out, and for a terrible moment he thought he would crash down into the room below. His fingers wanted to let go; his body could get no leverage.

With a huge effort he raised his head to the level of the opening, leaned forward, and rested some of his weight there. The metal edge cut into his forehead. His fingers seemed to break.

You are lifted, flying up into the blue space.
With Fabricon you will always be strong.

"Strong!" Tom shouted, and swung himself up on the ledge. He lay groaning in the darkness for a moment. The room, with its flashing lights, seemed miles below him.

He was in a vent, wide enough for him to crawl through. There was no problem deciding which way to go; he could not trust himself to swing across to the other side.

He began the slow crawl through the venting system. His overwhelming thought was that he'd escaped from the Pavlov Room.

One thing at a time, as his grandfather said.

He crawled forward through the darkness and saw a patterned light. He heard voices. He was coming to another room.

He knew he had to be careful. He was not sure how much noise he was making, or what would carry into the rooms below.

He flattened and crawled on his belly, inching forward and stopping, inching forward and stopping.

When he was over the vent he peered down but could see nothing. For a moment he stopped in a kind of terror. Voices came up to him, and one of them he recognized at once as Dr. Tarn's.

"Don't interrupt me, please," Tarn commanded.

"Why all this mumbo-jumbo?"

Tom felt a chill in his blood. The other voice sounded like … "We'll go in and see him in a minute. He'll be quite pacified, quite receptive. I'm counting on you to win him over. What he's up to is no good, but we can make a place for him."

"I don't understand how he went off the tracks like this."

Tarn chuckled and answered quickly. "I'm afraid he needs a father figure."

Tom suppressed a groan. He thought, *In a minute they'll be checking the room. I've got to get out of here.*

He continued his slow crawl; the tunnel went on. Where would it take him? How would he get out of there?

He was trying not to think of the voice of the second man.

Keep on moving, the answer was to keep on moving.

But the conversation came back to him. *It couldn't be. It just didn't make any sense.*

Another grid of light appeared before him. At the same time he heard voices behind him, muffled sounds, as if from the deep earth. The metal he was lying on began to shake. Voices sounded again, reverberating around him, hollow voices. He rolled over and looked back; he saw flashes of light, searching beams, in the deep maw behind him. They had found out his trick and were coming after him!

His whole world seemed to be collapsing. The grid went dark, then a light beamed up, blinding him. Whispered voices sounded close by.

Suddenly, the panel beneath him gave way. He started to fall, but rough hands seized him and he was held, dragged down. He twisted and kicked but they fastened his arms and held him. Someone shone a light in his face.

A familiar voice, the smooth voice of Tarn, his enemy, said, "Good work, gentleman. Now bring him into the next room. Our young friend's little adventure seems to be over."

CHAPTER SEVENTEEN

Father and Son

Tom stumbled forward. The room swayed around him. Two security guards, bulky men in grey overalls, pressed his arms tight behind his back. He squirmed away but they shook him until he held still. The light was blinding; he could smell their beer-sodden breath.

Dr. Tarn walked out of the shadows and stood in front of him. His white lab jacket seemed ruffled and ill-fitting, as if he had pulled it on too quickly. His blue eyes studied Tom as he spoke in a quiet voice.

"A very foolish move, Thomas. I gave you every chance and now you've betrayed me. You're a stupid boy, despite your costume and your tricks."

The other voice ... there had been someone in the room with Tarn.

Tom bent his glance away; he shook his head in a kind of protest. Though he wanted to challenge him, to denounce him, he knew he had to keep his mouth shut. He was also afraid. *Had Paul found the files? Had he made it out of the building?* If he had, they would be able to finish Tarn. Otherwise … he'd better not let on what he knew.

Tarn, for his part, was giving nothing away. "You know what this means, of course." He laughed shortly. "It means a felony charge and confinement in prison. And this time, no consideration."

He paused, as if to let this sink in, then continued. "I want to know exactly what led you to do this. Who your accomplices are and how this break-in was planned. Why are you wearing this ridiculous costume? Only yesterday I gave you good evidence as to how you were being mis-led and deceived. Some people have a lot to gain by dis-rupting Fabricon. You'll gain absolutely *nothing*."

Tom bent his glance. "I don't want to talk to you," he mumbled. *Did Tarn's questions mean that they hadn't caught Mercury Man? He couldn't be sure; he could only pray that it was so.* "I'll stand on my rights," he insisted. But his voice sounded choked and it bothered him.

"I haven't called the police yet, but I intend to," Tarn spoke dryly. He seemed to be studying the far wall. He looked at his watch and added, "I intend to give you one last chance, however."

Tom shrugged his shoulders, though his stomach was beginning to turn over.

"Take him down the hall!" Tarn ordered, and the guards shoved Tom through the doors and into the corridor.

Another guard waited there. When he saw Tom appear, he slipped by him and whispered something to

Tarn. The scientist pressed his lips together; Tom could not read his expression.

A few steps forward, then the guards pushed Tom through an open door and into another room, bare and brightly lit. The door slammed suddenly behind him; a man got up from behind a desk.

"Tom! What in hell's going on? I never thought you'd pull a stunt like this."

He hadn't heard wrong. He was here. His father was at Fabricon.

"Dad!" he said, but his heart was sinking.

Joe Blake was a tall, rugged man with greyish rough-cut hair and an easy smile. He was dressed in a blue suit that made him look uncomfortable; he wore no tie and his hands moved uncertainly as he spoke.

Tom could only stare at him, thinking how different he looked — not at all as he recollected. All his memory traces of his father seemed to be in close-up. He recalled his eyes and the curve of his mouth, his heavy eyebrows and his wrinkles. Now Tom seemed to be seeing him from a distance, from far away; it was as if the man had blurred or grown more awkward during all those years of absence.

When the moment of strangeness passed, anger came, and Tom pressed his lips together. This was the man who left them in poverty, who had caused his mother so much pain.

As if on a wrong cue, his father came forward and stuck his right hand out. Tom turned away, tried the door, but found it locked.

"I know you've got some hard feelings, son. It's been a hell of a long time."

"You didn't care!" Tom said fiercely. "You didn't care about us."

His father seemed uncertain. "Look, I didn't come here to defend myself. Tarn's boys got hold of me and told me you were in big trouble, so I came over to try to help. I know I haven't been the greatest father in the world, but I want to help you."

"He's using you, Dad, Tarn is using you. You don't know anything. They're probably monitoring us right now."

Joe Blake looked anxiously around, then smiled. "No! That's impossible! Why would he do such a thing? Son, I don't know the facts, but I want to help."

"He brought you here to confuse things. To get me out of his way. You don't know what he's doing! He's a madman! He's trying to destroy some friends of mine."

"Hey, just a minute! If he thinks I'll be fooled, he's crazy. I just want to make sure you don't get in trouble."

All of sudden Tom saw a gleam of hope. Could his father be telling the truth? Would anything be lost by confiding in him?

"You want to help? You really do?"

"Of course I do."

"Then get me out of here as quickly as possible."

His father looked abashed. "Now just a minute. As I understand it, you broke into this place. And for the second time, at that. If I help you get away I'll be assisting you to evade arrest. As a public servant, I can't afford to do that."

"You know something, Dad?"

"What?"

"You're full of crap."

Joe Blake flashed him an angry look. He took a step forward and stopped. Tom looked defiantly at his father, who continued in a subdued manner.

"There's no need for that kind of talk. Just tell me what's happened and why you're here and dressed in that crazy outfit. You can't fool around with these people, you know. This is a big corporation."

"Is that what they told you to tell me?"

"If you don't trust me, Tom, we're not going to get anywhere."

"All I want to do is to get out of here."

His father sighed, crossed the room, and sat down heavily behind the desk.

"I should never have come over here."

"Why did you?"

"I honestly wanted to help."

"What else did Tarn tell you?"

His father looked at him. "Nothing much. How's your mother, by the way?"

"Why didn't you call her once in a while to find out?"

"I did! I did — at the beginning. After a while she just wouldn't talk to me."

Tom swallowed. It sounded like his mother.

"How is she?"

"She's fine. She'll probably get married again."

He saw his father stir. "To the other guy? The guy in the weird suit?"

Tom started. He realized he hadn't thought of it. His mother and Paul — a strange idea! Then his hopes seemed to crash down. How did his father know about Paul?

"You mean you've seen Mercury Man? They've caught him?"

"Take it easy, son, they haven't caught anyone — except you. I heard those mugs mention the costumes. And who the hell's Mercury Man?"

"You mean he got away? Paul got away?"

"What are you talking about? You two were trying to rip the place off, is that it?"

"I can't believe it! Paul got away!"

"Were you trying to steal computer stuff? The two of you? That's what Tarn told me."

Tom sat up straight. "Tarn is a liar. He framed Paul because Paul found out he's making a super computer out of DNA material! And computer programs based on genetics. If he can get these on the market, there's no telling what might happen. Tarn thinks people are just fodder. You don't know him, Dad."

"You're not telling me you broke in here to foil a mad scientist?"

"That's exactly what we did, Dad!"

Joe Blake laughed tartly. "C'mon ... who's full of crap now?"

Tom sprang across the room; he stopped abruptly before the big desk and stood gazing down at his father.

Joe Blake returned his glance. That was more like it: close up, remembering.

"Dad! Get me out of here. This is serious! Help me. I wouldn't lie to you. You understand that?"

His father looked at him for a long time. His eyes seemed to grow heavy with recollection. He pressed his lips together and cleared his throat.

"You were always a pretty straight kid."

Tom turned away. He couldn't bear that his father should see his weakness. If his dad said another word he might just bawl. At that moment Tarn and all his tricks seemed to dwindle in importance.

"If I get you the hell out of here," Joe Blake said, "you'll tell me everything that happened?"

"If you swear not to tell Tarn."

"Why should I tell Tarn? Can't you trust me?"

"If you trust *me*."

His father paced across the room, not looking at him.

"What the hell!" he said, and slapped his son lightly on the arm. "You're getting to be a big son-of-bitch." He looked at Tom, smiled crookedly, and nodded.

Tom thought of the bulky guards outside the door. He pointed in their direction and made a gesture.

"I'll take care of them," his father said.

He waved Tom back, knocked on the door, and called out.

"Here, open this up, will you?"

Voices sounded outside. The door swung open.

Joe Blake pushed it back and stepped into the corridor, beckoning Tom to follow.

The guards eyed them, waiting for some explanation.

"I'm taking my son to the police station," Joe said. "That's what Dr. Tarn asked me to do."

Tom clenched his fists. Was his father playing it straight? Was this some kind of trick? He still wasn't sure he could trust him.

"I'm sorry, sir. We have orders to hold this boy. The company is going to charge him with breaking and entering."

"Let me speak to Dr. Tarn, then."

"I'm sorry, Dr. Tarn has left the building."

Tom exchanged a glance with his father.

"Now just a minute," Joe Blake went on. "You have no right to hold this boy here. Dr. Tarn designated me to take him to the station. If you won't let us go, I intend to call the police and then you'll have to take the consequences. The police chief is a very good friend of mine."

The guards shook their heads, but their faces were full of doubt. They withdrew a few steps down the corridor and began a whispered conversation. After a few minutes, one of them disappeared into a nearby room.

"He's going to phone," the other said.

Tom waited. His father was fingering an unlit cigarette. Then the first man came back, shrugging his shoulders. "All right," he said. "Take the kid away. He's in your hands, though, just remember that."

Tom couldn't believe his ears. They were letting him out of Fabricon!

His father led the way down the corridor. Neither of them looked back. A few doors opened as they passed by. Faces peered at them; Tom heard the low drone of conversations. An air of crisis seemed to have enveloped the building.

They emerged in the parking lot, and his father led the way to a shiny new red van, sitting by itself close to the entrance gate. Tom climbed into the front seat. In a few minutes they were out on Harbour Street.

"Where to?" his father asked.

"Just a few blocks," Tom explained. "So you're really not taking me to the station?"

"Of course not, not if I like your explanation."

"Pull over here and I'll try to fill you in."

They were directly opposite Mercury House. It looked shabby, hot, and blistered in the late afternoon sunlight. Tom thought with a thrill, *If all goes well I'll be seeing them all. But not there. We're supposed to meet in the tunnel.*

He took in the house and next to it the small dilapidated garage, which few would suspect was the entrance to a magical underworld. Down below, in a nuclear bunker that Zak Daniel had built in the fifties and later refurbished, they would be waiting for him.

He turned to his father and started to tell his story, leaving out a lot of things, most especially Miranda.

When he had finished, Joe Blake said excitedly, "Hell! I can't believe such a thing is going on in our city. There has to be a mistake in here somewhere."

"There's no mistake. You'll see! Paul has the evidence! I saw plenty myself!"

"Then, son, you've been playing with fire." His father sighed and shook his head. He seemed about to speak, then made a helpless gesture. "I'll do whatever I can to help you."

Tom waited for more. He felt uncomfortable with his father and wanted to get away. He could have jumped out of the van, but he resolved not to move. After everything, that would have been some kind of failure.

"I'm letting you go, Tom," his father announced at last. His stern tone seemed dutiful and not sincere. "That's because I believe you. And, after all, you're my kid. But if I find out you're lying, you'll be in trouble with me — I don't care what your mother says. I just hope you haven't chosen the wrong side."

Tom looked at the long, half-dilapidated porch of the old house. Was that a Siamese cat sitting on the cushionless swing beneath the bare twisted vines?

He turned suddenly to his father and asked, "Why did you leave us, Dad?"

His father didn't move or look at him. The question hung awhile in the silence. Finally, Joe Blake patted his son on the shoulder and said in a quiet voice, "Well, Tom, you're almost a grownup now. I believe you can take it. You see, there was this woman I met back then —"

A few minutes later, Tom stood alone on the street.

CHAPTER EIGHTEEN

Ad Astra

Tom walked along the ramp they had shown him the night before. Here the tunnel curved and the tracks wound away into the darkness. It hardly bothered him that the space was narrow, the lights dim, and the walls so close that he could touch the damp splotches on the bare rock and plaster. He had escaped from Fabricon, from the Pavlov Room with its horrors; he had seen his own father: tremendous events that caused him to stop more than once and contemplate everything afresh. It was as if he had walked into a new world.

The meeting with his father had shocked him. For years, he had thought of Joe Blake as remote and indifferent, but now he knew better. His father was friendly, blustering in his manner, and yet somehow unreachable. Tom felt guilty because he didn't like him better. Guilty about his own father! Yet his dad had talked about the past so casually — he seemed to expect Tom to forgive him the neglect of all those years after a handshake and a few jokes.

"Let's keep in touch, son," his father had said to him, leaning out of the van window. His smile seemed genuine, but also a little mechanical. Then he'd looked away quickly, as if Tom had read too much in his glance.

But Tom didn't want to keep in touch. It was all far too complicated! His father had been an absentee so long that Tom didn't know how to fit him into his life.

The sound of voices in the tunnel ahead broke in on his thoughts. His pulse quickened and he ran forward.

Now more than ever he needed to see them all, his new family.

There was light ahead, gigantic moving shadows: someone playing the beam of a flashlight against the tunnel walls.

And voices — *her voice in particular.*

"It's me!" he shouted and ran toward the light.

He sprinted around a corner. Miranda and his mother stood framed in a lighted passageway. When they saw him they jumped up and down and waved. They were almost the same height; he hadn't noticed that before.

"It's Tom!" his mother cried, and Miranda's voice sounded with hers, clear and beautiful.

The girl put down her light and ran toward him.

They hugged and held each other. Her body felt warm; he trembled with joy, feeling her so close.

"You've come back — and I can talk to you," she said.

"Miranda! Your voice is wonderful — just like I imagined it."

241

"Dad explained what happened. A reverse trauma, or something like that. You know after Fabricon's horrible programming I couldn't speak. Then, when I thought you'd been captured by Tarn, I just had to! I had so many ideas — of how we could rescue you."

"But, Miranda — your dad? He made it out?"

"Yes he did, thank God! And we've all been worried sick about you."

They walked arm in arm toward the bunker door. His mother watched them, then Paul came out and stood beside her.

Karen reached out, instinctively it seemed, and took Paul's arm. It was strange seeing his mother so comfortable with a man she'd just met. It didn't seem at all like her.

Zak Daniel appeared at the door, his wheelchair carefully poised at the top of a short ramp. He too was smiling.

Tom thought they were giving him quite a welcome, considering what a mess he'd made of things!

He and Miranda laughed together. Paul, subdued as usual, approached them.

"I'm surprised you want to stand so close to him," Paul said to his daughter. "He looks like something the cat dragged in."

Everyone laughed and Tom felt suddenly crushed — then Paul threw his arms around him and said in a quiet voice, "Good work, kid. Thanks to you I got the files out of there. How in hell did you get away?"

Tom gaped at him. "I was lucky," he mumbled. "I saw everything. You're right — there's a room, with images of all the kids! And diagrams of the brain ... I'm in there too!"

Tom felt Paul's arms around him. "Take it easy. It's over now. We're going to knock them for a loop." And after a pause, he added, "We were waiting for Jack. He's supposed to be bargaining for you right now. C'mon inside and relax. Then we can fill each other in."

"I'm proud of you, son," his mother told him. She hugged him and walked along holding his hand. Miranda ran ahead.

"I didn't do anything, Mom."

"You're here, aren't you? And you saved Paul, too — he says you did!"

They walked up the ramp and into the bunker. Despite the grim exterior, it seemed a cozy place. The ceilings were high, outfitted with fans and track lighting, and the walls were cleanly whitewashed. A few oriental rugs were scattered on the painted concrete floor. On one side were bookcases and two long tables covered with newspapers and magazines. On the other side Tom noticed a large sofa and armchairs. Coloured photographs brightened the walls, and there was a battery of equipment, including a television and a computer monitor, both turned on.

"We've been trying to get news of Fabricon," Zak explained. "But now you're here!"

Tom shook the old man's hand and crashed down on the sofa.

"Looks like the hero needs a drink," Zak said, flipping off the TV. Miranda disappeared through a door at the rear and returned with a small Coke and a bag of potato chips.

"We lack for nothing," Zak said. "Except news. How in blazes did you get away from Tarn?"

Tom took a drink, wiped his mouth, and looked doubtfully from face to face. The bunker was strange despite its homey touches; everything seemed too vivid, almost hallucinatory.

He turned quickly to Paul and said, "You got all the files — that's just great!"

"I got the files, all right," Paul said.

He walked over to the long table on which the TV sat and lifted a small black tubular object from a shoebox. He turned it around in his left hand, then connected it to the monitor on the table. Paul touched a keyboard and within seconds a set of complicated diagrams appeared on the screen.

These looked innocent enough, but other pages were more sinister: profiles of Tom and his friends, photographs, diagrams of their bodies, psychological information, lists of their friends and relations, and medical histories, as well as links to a world pool of information on DNA, mind control, and special programming.

"Wow! Lucky they didn't code this," Tom said.

"They did. What's lucky is they never changed the code! When I remembered that Tarn is one of those people who makes a copy of everything, and that he's a freak for storing things on Fabricon's new micro vault cylinders, I rummaged around and found this! I recognized the code at once — it would have meant nothing to an outsider. If we hadn't arrived in time the cylinders would have been tossed in the river."

"Tell Tom how you got out, Paul," his mother said.

Paul grinned. "It wasn't easy. The alarm went off and they had me trapped in the main lounge. Three guys appeared and I had no chance against them. Then two of them took off in a hurry. I guess you stirred up so much trouble they figured they were being invaded! That made the odds a little better and I managed to get out. I hopped the truck as planned and we came here. I wanted to go back for you, but then I remembered that if I had the files I could get anything I wanted from Tarn, including you!"

As Paul explained all this, Karen Blake was pacing up and down. She seemed to be reliving her worst fears. "Your grandfather went straight from Fabricon to his house," she said. "He's supposed to call the company. We thought he'd get you out of there. We haven't heard from him, though. We've been waiting."

"Matter of security," Zak explained. "He won't call us here — they might trace it."

"You escaped, that's the main thing," his mother continued. "What a clever guy!"

"I didn't exactly escape," Tom said. There was a pause. He felt them all looking at him. "I don't exactly know how to tell you …"

"Just tell us," Zak urged.

"My father got me out of Fabricon."

They looked at him. There was a moment's silence and then his mother burst out, "Your father! What does he have to do with it?"

"I didn't think you'd seen your father for years," Paul put in, looking from Tom to Karen Blake.

At the mention of Joe Blake, Karen seemed to lose her poise. "That pig! I should have known he'd turn up at the wrong moment!"

"If he rescued Tom, it was the right moment," Zak said quietly.

Tom took a deep breath. He'd been afraid of this. "I don't know exactly what happened ..." He looked at his mother, who was pressing Paul's hand, still trembling with anger. "All I know is that Tarn said he was going to charge me, have me thrown in jail. Then he took me to a room where Dad was waiting. We talked for a while and Dad got me out of there. He told the guards he was going to take me to the police. Tarn was gone by then."

Paul Daniel whistled softly.

"Didn't the creep explain why he was there?" Karen asked.

"He said Tarn got in touch with him. I think he was telling the truth, Mom. It's just what Tarn would do. He wanted to neutralize us, to get us out of the picture. He knew that we were working with Paul and Zak and he wanted to mess things up. He thought that if he brought Dad in he would throw me off the rails. He'd already started the process with the film he showed me yesterday."

"And of course your dad just breezed in, as Tarn knew he would. He must have checked up on him, too. But why did the jerk let you go?"

"He's my father, after all!" Tom paused; he was suddenly furious. They all looked at him. "I asked him to help and he did. Once Paul got the files they had to let me go. Mom, I didn't like Dad very much, but he helped me. He played it fair."

Zak nodded. "As you say, he's your father."

Tom pressed his lips together. It was no use talking about it. They wouldn't understand his feelings. But his mother put her arms around him.

"I know. Joe Blake is a great one for twisting things. I suppose he was full of sorrow, full of excuses ..."

Tom couldn't speak. He managed a nod and stared at the slowly turning ceiling fan.

Zak Daniel cleared his throat, spun his wheelchair around, and cackled like a mother hen. "By golly, who cares what he was full of? He helped get young Tom back here, didn't he?"

"So Binkley wasn't lying!" A voice from the doorway made them jump.

Paul sprang to his feet; Karen turned. Zak threw up his arms.

Tom got up and ran to embrace the smiling rotund figure who had walked into the bunker while they were talking.

"Grandpa! I got away! Everything's all right."

Jack nodded. "So I see! That's good news and I've got more of it! Luckily for you guys I wasn't the police. Didn't even close the door, eh? That's confidence!"

"The gang's all here! Thank goodness!" Zak called out.

"I've got plenty of news, but a glass of beer would make it flow better," Jack told them.

Tom sensed his excitement — they were all caught up in it.

Miranda fetched a beer. Jack swallowed a few mouthfuls, took a deep breath, and smiled. He flopped down on the sofa next to Tom. The others crowded around him.

Then Jack began to laugh. He opened his mouth as if to speak but seemed suddenly overwhelmed by the humour of everything. "Sorry ..." He apologized through his tears, wiped his face, sniffed, and told them, "Well, I just talked to the CEO Martin Binkley ..."

"Yeah? So what happened?" Zak bounced in his chair; he seemed ready to shake the news from him.

"Tell us!" Miranda said.

"To begin with, Tarn's out! He's leaving for Switzerland tonight."

The room erupted in a roar. Miranda squeezed Tom's hand. He raised it to his lips and kissed it. Then, half in embarrassment, he jumped up and did a kind of tap dance on the concrete floor.

When things settled down again, Jack told them, "We shouldn't be so ecstatic. That fellow's escaped and he's dangerous. Who knows who'll fund him the next time? All the same, we've got Binkley, and he's being very cooperative. He just brushed off the break-in, which is pretty good news. No question of reporting it to the police. He even made a joke about comic book heroes and said Fabricon could never hold a guy like Tom. Anyway, he wants to talk compensation for you, Paul, and for Miranda. He said he feared a grave injustice had been done. He referred to a *generous* compensation, in fact."

Paul laughed shortly. Zak said, "Damned right!"

"That's just wonderful," Karen Blake said. She hugged Paul and her father and kissed Miranda, then stood holding Tom's hand. They all waited as Jack continued.

"Binkley promised that all Fabricon programs would be re-evaluated, and if any irregularities were found things would be fixed and people would be compensated. As I read it, that's company jargon that really means: 'I know we screwed up and we're going to fix it!'"

"That means the kids will learn the truth," Tom said. "They've got to be compensated, too. Listen, Grandpa! I saw their secret room. I broke in there. Binkley must have known. I want to talk to the lawyer before they destroy the evidence!"

"Don't worry, Tom," Paul reassured him. "There's plenty of evidence on that cylinder I lifted from them! And the hard files — which they probably will be too scared to destroy now — even show several models of the kids' brain charts. The whole process is there. And some very incriminating memos from Binkley. I suspect we'll be getting him tossed out of Fabricon as well!"

"Well, he's already covering his ass." Jack laughed. "Binkley told me that the idea of unmonitored genetic experiments was abhorrent to him. He actually used the word *abhorrent*. More company jargon, but I think we can feel good about the result."

"It won't do him any good," Paul said. He seemed subdued and didn't look at any of them. "I've got the files and Tarn knew he was finished. All that playing around to try to stop us — bringing in your father, Tom — it meant nothing once we got the files. And now they'll have to come through. They'll have to make good on this."

"I don't think there's any question about it," Jack said. "Binkley even mentioned something like scholarships for Tom and Miranda. That lawyer you put me on to is going to see their lawyers tomorrow. He thinks we have them by the — He thinks they're over a barrel, all right."

Paul Daniel laughed grimly. "We'll have to get guarantees. They'll be lucky to keep the company afloat after this. They might all be in jail — where they belong — or the company may be totally discredited. But maybe the good people in the corporation — if any turn up — can get rid of the rats without sinking the ship, if you see what I mean, Jack."

"That's what will surely happen!" Zak told them. "Fabricon is worth saving, and it'll be worth millions to us when they do save it. We can set up the park again. We can all work together on it! Marvin would have loved this — and my own Mary. We'll finally be in business again! Hell, if we had an artist, we could even begin another series of comics — a new Mercury Man."

"You do have an artist," Jack announced. "From what I've seen you've got a very good artist. I'll leave you to guess who it is."

"Grandpa!" Tom got up and paced across the floor.

"Mercury Man and Tom Strong!" Jack crowed. "I think I'll have another beer. I want to toast the big heroes of the day. And the heroes of the future."

Tom fetched the beer for his grandfather. Jack raised his glass and smiled. Tom noticed that his mother was in close conversation with Paul Daniel. He had to admit that they looked awfully good together.

Miranda had noticed it, too, and she smiled at him.

"We have to go find the kids," Tom told her. "Grandpa will get in touch with them and their parents, but we should see them right away."

Miranda nodded and led the way quietly out of the bunker.

The tunnel was silent, strange. They nuzzled close, making slow progress, but following the tracks along through the half-darkness. They seemed to float along together. Tom felt as if his body and soul were dissolving in pure happiness.

They came at last to a passageway, dimly lit by a small red sign that said: "EXIT."

There was an elevator. Miranda pressed the button and it clanked down the shaft to them. The doors opened and they entered. As they rode up, Miranda said, "Please give me back the ring now."

He looked at her in astonishment. She spoke slowly and carefully, but every word was clear.

He contemplated his ragged costume, thinking how bedraggled and foolish he looked. One glove was gone, along with his mask, while his jersey was torn and blackened with dirt from his experience in the venting shafts. Tom Strong hadn't done much! His father had saved him by bluffing his way out, and Tarn had simply disappeared. He didn't feel like much of a hero after all. Even so …

"Give you back the ring? But why, Miranda?" he pleaded with her. "I mean … I don't ever want to give it up."

She smiled. "You don't need the ring now. You've got me. I'll give it back to you if I ever think you need it."

Tom looked at her doubtfully, hesitated, then worked the ring off his finger and gave it to her. He was stunned. "I guess I'm not Tom Strong any more," he said, feeling more than a little crestfallen.

But Miranda stroked his cheek and said, "You are Tom Strong — and Mercury Man, too!" She kissed him until he shivered with joy. "You've always been Tom Strong — you just didn't know it."

The elevator doors opened. They were in another tunnel, but clearly no longer underground. Miranda led the way to the actual exit. In a few minutes they stood in Harbour Street, beside the dilapidated shed and next to Mercury House, where so many things were about to change.

Night had fallen over West Hope. A few early stars were visible, not quite extinguished by the lights of Fabricon, towering above the other buildings.

Then a Siamese cat appeared, crawling out from under an overturned wheelbarrow and into the lighted space beside them. He waited patiently while Tom and Miranda bent down together to stroke him. But after a while he crept away, gazing back at them only once with his enigmatic blue eyes.